Becoming Afua Osei

BIPOLAR DISORDER CHANGED MY LIFE

MARY MENSAH

Contents

Mary Mensah

Content Warning:
Becoming Afua Osei contains issues with mental illness including hospitalization. Read chapter 7 at your own risk.

Book design by Sjayartisry

ISBN (Paperback) 979-8-9904062-3-0
ISBN (eBook) 979-8-9904062-0-9

This book is dedicated to my family for always believing in me and supporting me in my endeavors. They always tell me to reach my goals even when I feel discouraged and want to give up. This is also for anyone who is struggling with mental illness. You are not alone in all this.

New Beginnings

THIS WASN'T SUPPOSED TO HAPPEN TO ME. WHY DID IT FEEL LIKE I WAS going down a dark place? I could hear it now, *you are crazy!* Those words killed me inside, because I was labeled before people even got to know me. Bipolar disorder? Depression? How could this happen to me? I was definitely dreaming. This must be a bad nightmare. Wake up! This wasn't normal.

If you're wondering how it all started, let me introduce myself and take you back.

My name is Afua Osei, and most people would consider me an introvert. I mean, what can I say, I love my solitude. While most people were off partying and going to clubs, I preferred to stay indoors with a good show or book. Currently, I'm watching my favorite show called *A Different World.* Even though I was not born in the 90s, I loved this show because it had black people who were trying to excel in life. My favorite person on the show was Kim because she fought against all the odds to become a doctor.

Since I was a child, I'd always been different from the crowd. I was enrolled in the gifted and talented program at my school because my teachers said I was advanced for my age. I loved learning about different things and always took school seriously. One of my teachers in first grade, Mrs. Williams, saw something in me. She pushed me to read books and would often give me books to take home.

I would often finish one book a week. That's where my love for books came from. My parents came from a country in West Africa called Ghana. Not to brag, but it's the best place to be. I traveled there when I was ten and I had the most fun I've ever had in my life. We went to Labadi Beach and ate some amazing food. I recalled eating jollof rice and goat meat. It was so delicious. My parents took me to the places they'd been to in the city of Accra, which is the capital of Ghana. I even went to the slave castle in Elmina. It was eye-opening to see all that people went through when they were sold into slavery. Seeing it made me cry because they were in a cramped room and taken to a ship to a foreign country, where they had to assimilate.

Everyone was friendly in Ghana; I guess that was why we were known for being the most peaceful in all of Africa. My parents always wanted what was best for me. They helped me foster my gift. My parents used to say, "Nyame boa nea oboa ne ho," which meant God helps those who help themselves. I remembered them telling me stories of when they were in Ghana. On one occasion, I remembered my dad talking about going to the farm to help his mother. Then having to sell some food before going to school.

I cherished those stories because they motivated me to try my best. My grandfather on my mom's side used to be a principal. He always advocated for education and would gladly help his students so that they could excel. I guess that rubbed off on me because I would one day want to be an educator. Well, after I get my PhD and become a psychotherapist.

I would love to become a professor and help future therapists. I know, a little overambitious, but a girl can dream. I knew this was what I wanted to be for quite some time. When I was in high school, I shadowed a psychotherapist at her private practice. Her name was Dr. Franklin. She was amazing. I remembered her encouraging me to follow my dreams. I sat in on one session she had with a client that gave permission.

I remembered her using reflection, a technique that involved the therapist paraphrasing what the client said to make them feel heard and understood. After that day, I knew this was what I wanted to become in the future. I knew if I wanted to become a psychotherapist, I would have to get good grades, which wasn't hard for me to do. Throughout my whole high school career, I got straight A's.

I was in an honors program. We used to do community service projects around New York City. In one instance, we went to Prospect Park to help clean up the litter. It was during that time that I met my best friend, Veronica Diallo. She was also African; her parents came originally from Senegal. She was very petite and had almond-shaped eyes. Veronica and I were practically attached at the hip. When you saw me, you saw her. We meshed so well. We even had the same taste in music. We both loved African music. Our favorite artist was Burna Boy. We could gist all day about popular African artists.

She wanted to become a medical doctor and had been preparing for it since freshman year of high school. When I tell you this woman worked hard. I really meant it; even when I wanted to give up, her work ethic motivated me. She ended up being accepted into the Macaulay Honors program for CUNY. She decided to go to Hunter College, which had an amazing biology program. I was beyond ecstatic for her.

Most people in my school went to prom, but I didn't because I felt it was a waste of time. Looking back, I wish I went for the experience. I graduated as the valedictorian from Telecommunications High School in Brooklyn, New York. I wrote a speech that came from my heart. I used an African proverb that said, "If you want to go fast, go alone. If you want to go far, go together." This talked about teamwork and how it's essential to succeed in life. My parents were the reason I got to this point in my journey. If I didn't have their support and that of my peers, who knows where I'd be. My parents would later tell me how proud they were of me.

That year, I got accepted into my dream school, which was SUNY Albany. Guess what? I got a full ride to that school because of my hard work and persistence. I chose this school because it had a good psychology department. Plus, they also had PhD programs that might be of interest to me later. I was happy to be on my own for the first time.

I had three other siblings, one brother and two sisters. I was the oldest. I loved them with all my heart, but I just needed my space. Even though my siblings and I got along, I needed my freedom so I could be more independent. I didn't mean to sound ungrateful, but the older I got, the more I craved my alone time. School started in August of 2022. I remembered buying so many things at Walmart, Marshall's, and Target.

I watched more than enough dorm room tours on YouTube. I was prepared! I recalled the drive up to Albany; it was about three hours. I was so excited to finally have freedom. That first day, I settled into my dorm room. My parents helped me decorate. As many people knew, my favorite color was pink. So, you could only imagine how good it looked. I had satin lined pink pillowcases. A fluffy pink throw pillow. Some light pink sheets and pink accessories to match. When I tell you my room was decked out, it truly was.

Let's talk about my amazing roommate. Can you tell I'm being sarcastic? Let's take it back to when we first communicated with one another. My school had a housing portal that told you who your roommate would be for the school year. I checked the portal one day and saw that I was matched with a girl named Melissa Marzano. I immediately looked her up on Facebook and sent her a friend request. We chatted and got to know each other.

She was from Staten Island in a town called Waverly Place. Melissa had long brunette hair and rosy cheeks. She also had a very athletic build and wore braces. In her spare time, she played women's hockey. I thought we would be good friends. I really did, and it was odd because we talked almost every week leading up until move-in day. The day I arrived at my dorm, my roommate didn't greet me. She wasn't even happy I arrived. My parents noticed it too, but didn't say anything. I knew from then on that my roommate and I wouldn't be the best of friends. It was understandable because I heard that your roommate would most likely not be your friend long-term.

When my parents invited my roommate to come and pray with us, she said no. Then she proceeded to walk out the room without saying anything. My parents questioned it, saying how rude she was. I knew she wasn't obligated to pray with us. Maybe she had a different religious belief. Regardless, she could've been kinder. My parent wanted me to move out, but I insisted on staying. I told them that she would change, maybe she was homesick. I should've just moved out, because what would later happen changed the way I saw her.

After my parents prayed, we finished setting up my side of the room. We later went to a local restaurant to eat called Mi Vida, which in Spanish translates to *my life*. It was nice being able to hang out with my family for the last time. We ate some amazing food. I remembered we all had their beef tacos, which were so delicious. My father drove me back to my dorm. My parents hugged me and advised me to be careful with my roommate.

As I walked to my dorm, disappointment filled my body as I returned to my dorm because I'd be alone with a roommate that I disliked. That was when I bumped into this guy. I would later come to find out his name was Jeremy Alexander. I was so lost in thought that I didn't notice him.

I immediately said, "OMG! I'm so sorry."

He accepted my apology, to my surprise. New Yorkers tended to have attitudes when they felt disrespected.

"What's your name?" he said, looking at me intently, waiting for a response. I suddenly froze. I wasn't sure what it was, really. I thought it was nervousness. My stomach turned and I was unable to speak. He proceeded to ask me again. I was back to myself.

I nervously said, "My name is Afua."

He said, "You finally answered! For a second, I thought something was wrong." He was tall and dark-skinned with a full beard and a nice haircut. He had this beautiful smile. He had this sparkle in his eyes.

Jeremy asked me what I was doing later. I told him that I had nothing planned, that I was a freshman and didn't know anyone.

He laughed and said, "I figured you were a freshman or a transfer student, because I've never seen you around."

Jeremy invited me to hang out with him and his friends later that day. We exchanged numbers. As he left, I felt butterflies in my stomach. You know I had to call my best friend and share this gist with her.

I walked to my dorm room and look who I saw, Melissa. She was in the room and as I walked in, she just looked at me. I said hello and she just stared at me in disgust. At that moment, I didn't know what to do. I brushed it off, because no one was going to ruin my mood. I mean, I just met a handsome guy, and he invited me to hang out with him.

The reason why I was happy about this encounter was because, for once, a guy wasn't afraid to talk to me. In high school, nobody looked my way. I overheard once that a guy was intimidated to talk to me because I was so smart. He said he'd date me, but would feel inferior around me. After that day, I stopped paying attention to the guys at my school. As you know by now, I had African parents. Why did that matter, you might ask?

Well, my parents always told me education came first. They said

I couldn't date until I was eighteen. I mean, that was better than some people. My aunt told my mom I shouldn't date until I'm twenty-five. I thought, *what does my aunt know about dating nowadays?* My mom laughed and said I could date when I was ready, but preferably after I turned eighteen. My dad, on the other hand, refused to believe that I was growing up. It's like he never wanted me to date. How crazy was that?

I sat on my bed and called my friend Veronica. She was so happy to hear from me. "Afua, how are you? Last we spoke, you were buying things for your dorm. How are things with your roomie?"

I decided to lie and say everything was fine just to keep the peace.

Veronica, knowing me so well, sensed something was up. "Sis, I can hear it in your voice something is wrong. When you are frustrated, your voice has a higher pitch. Is everything okay?"

Deep down inside, I wanted to tell her how horrible Melissa was being towards me. "Nothing is wrong with me, I must be feeling a little homesick. "I could tell Veronica wanted to discuss that further, but she stopped in her tracks. Instead, I switched the topic. "So, I met a guy named Jeremy and I think he's really cool."

"OMG, I'm so happy for you! I think you should wait for him to make the first move and text you first, before meeting up with him." She said I shouldn't be afraid of talking to guys, because one day I'd be dating. We talked for over an hour about other things, but she had to do chores, so we said bye to one another.

I was sitting in my room, wondering when Jeremy would text me. Thirty minutes passed before I got a text. He said, "Hey this is Jeremy, the guy you bumped into. Do you have anything planned for the night?"

I was overwhelmed with excitement. I mean, a girl like me getting a guy's attention was interesting. "I have nothing planned for the rest of day," I said.

"Why don't you meet me in the main lounge. That's if it's alright with you?"

"Of course we can meet up." I texted, holding back my excitement. I immediately jumped out of my bed and headed straight to the lounge. My heart was skipping a beat. I was nervous.

When I entered the lounge, I saw him watching *Game of Thrones*. There were people on the other side, playing what appeared to be Uno. As soon as Jeremy saw me, his face lit up with excitement. There was that beautiful smile I fell in love with. I felt butterflies all over again. I didn't know if it was a good or bad thing. He got up and gave me the biggest hug ever. He smelled so good. The smell reminded me of One Million by Paco Rabanne.

We sat down on the couch and got comfortable. "Afua, what do you like to do for fun?" Jeremy asked.

"Well, I enjoy reading and watching TV in my spare time," I replied. "What about you?"

"I am into hiking, and I do that with my family every summer."

We started discussing facts about one another. His parents were originally from Trinidad and lived in Queens. They immigrated from Trinidad before Jeremy was born. He said that he loved Brooklyn and would often travel to see his cousins. They went to concerts at the Barclays Center.

We bonded over the fact that we both had three other siblings.

"What part of Africa are your parents from?" Jeremy asked.

"My parents are from Ghana which, fun fact, it's known as the Gold Coast because it's a large supplier of gold."

"Wow, you know your history. I know about some Ghanaian artists. My favorite is King Promise," he said enthusiastically.

I thought to myself, *This guy is cultured and knows about things beyond his scope.*

He told me he was a sophomore in the chemistry program and would one day want to become a chemist. As he spoke, his face lit up and was relaxed. He seemed very passionate as he talked about why he chose the field. That excitement made me want to learn more about him.

"I was interested in science ever since I was eight years old. I would also read science books to gain more knowledge," he said.

Immediately I was intrigued, because I considered myself a sapiosexual, which meant I found intellect attractive in a person.

"I have big dreams of becoming a therapist, preferably opening my own private practice. I see a need of mental health services for minority communities. I usually see that people don't take mental health seriously. I want to break the stigma of mental illness and prove that we all can get help."

He looked at me with intention and said, "I can tell you're really passionate about this. Keep going, and you will accomplish your goals with faith."

I told him that I dreamed of this since high school, when I shadowed a therapist. Jeremy told me that he liked that I was ambitious and that I wanted to help people.

We had been talking for over two hours when we realized it was getting late. He decided to walk me to my dorm and hugged me goodbye.

As we walked to my room, I felt this growing sense of happiness. That would soon fade once I went inside my room.

Before I could say anything, Melissa said, "Where were you?"

Excuse me, but you're not my parent. I don't have to explain myself to you. I wanted to tell her off because all day she'd been giving me attitude. I just ignored her and went straight to my bed. I didn't feel like explaining my whereabouts to her. As I sat on my bed, all the self-defeating thoughts started trickling in my mind. I thought about how a guy like Jeremy could fall in love with me.

One thing about me: I overthought and analyzed everything. It could be to my detriment at times. I mean, look at me, how can any man fall for me? I was 5'6" and so skinny for my height. I wasn't always this way. Like two years ago, I was at my heaviest I'd ever been. I weighed around two hundred pounds. I overheard a family friend commenting on my weight and skin color. When I was in close proximity to them, they began telling me I'd grown fat.

They said, "Wow, Afua wayɛ kɛse. What happened to you, you've gotten fat. This isn't good, reduce your food intake, okay?"

After that day, I began to be self-conscious about my looks. I mean why wouldn't I, they embarrassed me. It's sad that even members of your own race could make such colorist and fatphobic comments about you.

I developed an eating disorder. I wouldn't eat for days on end. Whenever I ate, I would exercise immediately after. If I ate too much on a certain day, I would work out for hours to burn off the calories. I thought about purging, but was too scared. Plus, I hated the smell or taste of vomit. It wasn't until I collapsed one day that my view on my body changed. I was hospitalized for three days. Doctors said I was dehydrated. My mom talked to me about how dangerous that was for me to do. She didn't realize I was dealing with an eating disorder. After that day, I vowed not to do that again. It wasn't easy, because I almost relapsed a few times.

I thought about the eventful day I had. It wasn't all bad; I mean, I got to hang out with my parents and I made a new friend. I realized I forgot to call my parents to see if they arrived home.

I called my mom because I figured my dad was driving and didn't need to be distracted. My mom answered and she said that they were thirty minutes away from our house. They would've been home sooner, but they made a rest stop. She asked me if things got better with my roommate. To keep the peace, I lied and said everything was fine. She warned me to be careful in college and watch out for my roommate. After that, she prayed for me. I didn't remember falling asleep. I guess I was tired.

Start of Something

Wake up! Wake up! I told myself. My body was fighting getting up, but the sound of my alarm finally got me out of bed. It was a Saturday, and it hit me that I was in college and would be there for quite some time. I would miss my family and everything I knew. School would start in two days. Before I could even check my phone, Melissa asked if she could talk to me. I just ignored her and checked my phone.

"I can see that you don't want to talk right now." I guess my face said it all. "I'm so sorry Afua, for how I treated you."

I kept listening but honestly, I didn't believe her. "I was mad at my boyfriend Todd because he hasn't spoken to me in over three days. Anytime I would call him, it would go straight to voicemail. I have been calling him nonstop and I'm growing irritated. I bet he's with some other girl and purposely ignoring me." Melissa kept on talking. I felt sympathy for her at that moment. "We had a big argument about him coming to see me. He's being very inconsiderate of my feelings, being that he has a car and can easily come to see me. Meanwhile, I have to take a bus followed by a train. He was complaining about the commute to the school. He said it's simply too long of a drive. Can you believe that?"

It must be difficult to have a boyfriend treat you like that. I was thinking how he must be a big piece of trash. Another thing you should know about me: I give people second chances because we all make mistakes. She seemed sincere. I wanted to believe she would change.

I waited for her to finish complaining about Todd. Then I checked my phone. Guess who texted me? It was Jeremy, he sent me a good morning text. He wanted to know if I could have breakfast with him at the dining hall. I texted him and said I'd be ready by nine. I got up, showered, and got ready to meet him. We decided to meet in the main lobby near the front desk of our dorm. When I saw him waiting at the lobby, I instantly felt a warm presence, like I could trust this guy. I called his name and instantly, he greeted me with a smile and a hug.

We walked to the dining hall and immediately there was a lady greeting us, asking for our ID. She said we were a cute couple. I immediately felt shy. Deep down inside, I felt like it would be true one day. I wondered if he felt the same way about me. We ended up just laughing it off. I hadn't gotten my student ID yet because the student services center wasn't open on weekends. Jeremy used his guest swipes on me, which I appreciated. When I entered, I saw a wide array of food. There weren't too many people up this early.

We both got some eggs, bacon, and hash browns. For my drink I got cranberry juice, while Jeremy got orange juice. We found a nice place to sit down near a window.

"If I may ask, what's your dating life like?" Jeremy said, clearing his throat shortly after.

My stomach began to turn at the thought of that question.

Surely, he'd think I was weird. I paused and said, "I have actually never dated or had a boyfriend before."

He looked at me in surprise and said, "Really? I thought you would have by now. But I get it, dating is hard."

I was glad he understood where I was coming from. "I have African parents and they do not play about dating. They always say no boyfriend because you'll get pregnant, and we'll send you on a plane to Ghana. My mom said I can date once I reach eighteen."

He was very understanding and nonjudgmental. That's what I liked about him. He was great at conversation. I felt as though I knew him my whole life.

I asked him the same question, to which he replied, "My last relationship was a year ago." He told me how the girl wasn't ambitious and thought he was too boring because he loved learning. She was also insecure because he was getting attention from other women, and she thought he'd cheat on her. Eventually things got rocky, and they ended the relationship, but she was still in love with him. He said he wanted nothing to do with her because she tried to ruin his life. She spread some awful rumors about him that nearly ruined his reputation.

I thought, *wow what a shame*, because so far, he'd been a gentleman towards me. I wanted to let him know that I was different without sounding like a pick-me. I ended up not saying anything because he wasn't my boyfriend and I don't want to come off as desperate.

After we finished eating, we walked back to the dorm. As we were walking, we saw that the school was setting up activities for the students. There was a bouncy house. I saw a big sign that said, "Carnival For All." As we approached the area, we saw a sign saying that it started at 12:30 pm. We decided that we would meet up later to go. Jeremy said he'd invite some of his friends to join us in the festivities. He suggested that I invite my roommate. I contemplated on telling her. I later figured that inviting her would allow her to get over Todd and his antics.

As I returned to my room, I couldn't stop thinking about Jeremy and how sweet it was talking to him. I entered my room to find that Melissa wasn't there. I decided at that moment I'd call Veronica and tell her all that happened. I told her that Jeremy asked me to eat breakfast with him.

She said, "Girl, I think he likes you."

"Maybe, but I think it's too early to say for sure." Both Veronica and I hadn't been in a real relationship. Veronica did go on a date once that ended terribly. Basically, the guy wanted her to pay for both of their meals. Meanwhile, he was the one that asked her on the date. If you're broke, just say that. No need to be going on dates you couldn't afford.

So, we didn't have much to base things off other than romance movies and books. We were hopeless romantics and lived for moments like this.

"One of the dining hall staff told us we were a cute couple," I added.

Veronica screamed, "OMG, I think that's a sign!"

I just laughed because I was nervous and didn't know what to say. Thinking about relationships scared me. What if I made a mistake and he wanted nothing to do with me?

"Sis, come on. You need to get out of your own head and start thinking positively," Veronica said.

"Jeremy has an ex that's still in love with him, but he assured me that he wants nothing to do with her. So that could be trouble," I explained.

She said, "I hope that ex of his does not cause trouble for you, if things progress into a relationship."

I was so sure that I wouldn't encounter issues, because for one she didn't know me, but I could be wrong.

Veronica and I talked on the phone about a lot of things. We were both sharing our nervousness about starting school in two days. It would be a whole new world for us. I was a bit sad that I wouldn't have my best friend by my side at school. We shared the same sense of humor and had inside jokes that only we understood. We had this habit of creating nicknames for guys that we liked. I hadn't created a nickname for Jeremy yet.

As I thought about how this school year would be, I got nervous all over again. I knew we would be successful because we were intelligent and driven individuals. College could be hard, but we'd come too far to let our parents down. Speaking of my parents, I forgot to call them. I let Veronica know I must call my parents. We ended the phone call with inspirational words to one another.

When I called my mom, she immediately answered with, "How come you didn't call me sooner?"

"I ate breakfast with a new friend I made," I explained.

"Oh, and who is this new friend?" she inquired. I finally told her it was a guy and she lit up in excitement. She said, "Is this a guy you like?"

I felt uncomfortable talking about dating with my mom sometimes because she usually overreacted. "Maybe," I said. That was when the lecture came.

"You need to be careful of these men, my darling, you never know what they've got going on. For all you know, he could be a player wasting your time," my mom warned me. "You need to practice discernment with anyone you even think about dating."

I listened to her advice because my mom was looking out for my best interest. I asked to speak to my dad. She gave him the phone and he immediately asked about how things were going with my roommate.

"She apologized," I told him.

"Still, be careful. School should always come first, Afua." My dad always gave me a speech about doing well in school. That I was a representation of our family and I shouldn't let them down. It wouldn't be my dad without a good lecture.

After I got off the phone with my parents, I laid in my bed. I was bored out of my mind. I wondered what happened to Melissa. Twenty minutes passed by and I got a knock on my door. It was my RA, which is short for Resident Assistant. Her name was Stacy. She introduced herself to me. She invited me to come to the main lounge at 8 pm. She wanted to formally introduce herself to the people that lived on the floor. Stacy was so beautiful. She had this big afro and flawless brown skin. She was very curvy. Stacy had a kind demeanor about her.

I almost forgot that Jeremy said I should meet him at the lobby by 12:30 pm. I checked my phone to see a text message from him. He said he was waiting at the same place we met up earlier. He was with two friends, Gabriel and Alyssa. As I walked to the main lobby, I was nervous because I hoped his friends would like me. When I arrived, Jeremy gave me a big hug and then introduced me to his friends. Gabriel was also tall, but lighter in complexion. He had hazel eyes. Alyssa was Dominican and had big curly hair. She had big brown eyes. They both greeted me with a warm hug as well and instantly, I felt comfortable around them.

"What happened to your roommate?" Jeremy asked.

"I haven't seen her since we left for breakfast."

He frowned a bit. "That's odd. But maybe she just went somewhere," he added, dismissing it.

We headed to the carnival and immediately, I was happy. There was so much stuff to do. There was a bouncy house, cartoonist, pin making station, popcorn/ice-cream station, stuffed animal station, etc. I didn't even know where to go first. I ended up heading towards the stuffed animal station because I saw a long line forming.

As I waited in line, I start a conversation with Jeremy and his friends.

"Does UAlbany normally have events like this?" I said.

In unison, they replied with yes. It made me chuckle a little, which made us all laugh.

Alyssa chimed in, "They have yearly carnivals for the students who are newcomers like yourself. The school also has other events from different organizations on campus. They are really fun too. Girl, you'll love it at school."

"I am a part of the Caribbean Student Association (CSA), and the Chemistry Club," Jeremy said to me.

Gabriel made it known that he was part of the African Student Organization (ASO).

"Afua, since you're African, would you mind joining ASO?"

I thought about reinventing myself, and being involved on campus was a good start. "I'll let you know, Gabriel," I said. I learned that he was from Liberia.

"I am in the Curly Hair Club and think you should join because we talk about self-love and embracing our natural hair." As Alyssa said this, she was smiling and twirling her hair. I marveled at how beautiful her hair was. It looked healthy and long. I realized that they were all active on campus. Since they convinced me, I was thinking about joining ASO and the Curly Hair Club.

As time passed, the line got shorter and it became our turn to get stuffed animals. They had four different kinds of animals. There was a lion, teddy bear, elephant, and giraffe. I chose the teddy bear and the person at the station started stuffing it with cotton. There was also an option to put a voice message inside, just like Build-A-Bear Workshop. I put something motivational such as *love yourself first*. Jeremy got a lion, but he didn't get it for himself, it was for his youngest sister Naomi which I thought was so adorable of him to do. He put a message that said, "I love you." Alyssa got what she wanted as well. I believe it was also a teddy bear. Gabriel didn't get anything, saying he didn't want one.

We headed over to the cartoonist. There was a big line forming for that too.

As we waited, we started talking about how this semester would be.

"I am nervous about starting school soon. There will be a lot more expected out of me," I said.

They assured me that if I found a balance between my personal life and school, I should be fine. That's when I found that they all had jobs on campus. Gabriel and Alyssa both worked at Tim Horton's, while Jeremy worked at the international office. I thought about getting a job because I'd rather make my own money than depend on my parents. My parents sacrificed so much for me. Before we knew it, it was our turn to see the cartoonist. It was a lady with red hair.

She told us, "Two people at a time."

Jeremy and I decided to get drawn together while Gabriel and Alyssa waited in line. It was cool sitting next to Jeremy. The cartoonist said we should relax and just smile. We sat there for a couple minutes and before we knew it, she was done drawing us. We both looked at the drawing in amazement. She was talented. We waited for Alyssa and Gabriel by the popcorn and ice cream station. A few minutes later, they joined us. We all talked about how cool the drawings looked. We got our popcorn and ice cream and decided to eat the ice cream before it melted. Afterwards, we watched a movie in our lounge since it was getting late.

As we entered the dorm and headed to the lounge, we saw a few people moving in their stuff. This weekend, tons of students would be settling in. It was the weekend before school started, which made sense. I noticed how hectic it was. There were a few RAs standing there to check the students in. I didn't recall seeing some of these people before. When I checked in, I had another girl named Sandra. She had blonde hair and blue eyes. She was nice to me. I hadn't seen her since I moved in. I guessed she was an RA from another dorm helping out. I spot my RA, Stacy, who waved in my direction, and I waved back.

Jeremy said we should put our stuff in the dorm room and meet up to watch a movie. As I walked to my dorm, I kept thinking about what happened to Melissa. I opened the door to my room to find that Melissa was still not there. I decided to text her. She told me that

Todd came to surprise her at the school. They made up and were no longer arguing. He decided to take her to the mall. I told her that we had a meeting with the RA at 8 pm. After that I put my teddy bear and cartoon drawing on my bed, then headed to the lounge. Jeremy and his friends were already in the lounge.

They were waiting for me so that we could agree on a movie to watch on Netflix. We decided upon watching *Love and Basketball.* I watched it before, and it was a nice movie. We were really enjoying the movie. We got to the part where Monica and Quincy played basketball together. In the scene, Monica was trying to win Quincy's heart. They had been broken up for some time. I thought that was beautiful, how people fought for the love they wanted. But how Quincy treated Monica like she was nothing to him showed me all I needed to know about some men. I mean, their love story wasn't perfect, but they eventually got together. It showed struggle love, to be honest. It was entertaining, but at what cost? She had to play for his love. I thought about Jeremy and I. How much I wanted to be in a relationship with him. I hoped he felt the same way about me. I wanted our own love story. One without struggle and pain. That was when I checked and it was almost time for my floor meeting with Stacy.

The movie ended and I told Jeremy and his friends that I had a floor meeting with my RA, Stacy. Alyssa told me she knew Stacy because she was the president of Curly Hair Club. I wondered how she balanced doing multiple things on campus. Alyssa said that she was very kind, and I would like her. They left for their own room. While I just waited for the meeting to start, I saw a bunch of people coming to the lounge. I finally saw Melissa and she was with a tall guy with short brunette hair. She was smiling from ear to ear. He left and she walked towards me.

Melissa came to sit next to me. "You won't believe this—Todd finally came to visit me!" she exclaimed.

"I'm so happy for you," I said, although I wondered why she didn't bother introducing me to him. Maybe she would later.

"What's this meeting about, anyway?" Melissa asked. I told her that the RA was going to introduce herself to us. A little while later, I saw Stacy coming to the lounge with another RA.

"Hi everyone, my name is Stacy."

"My name is Devin, and we will be your RAs for the school year." They tell us the rules that we must obey and follow.

"One of the rules you must follow is no drinking in the dorms if you're under 21," Stacy said. "The last time someone underage drank, they got into so much trouble, which was unfortunate," she continued.

"You will have a roommate agreement form that needs to be filled out by the end of the week," Devin said. The form was for us to create rules that Melissa and I would agree upon. Such as sleeping schedules, study times, and overnight guests. This was important so that we could minimize disagreements with one another.

"Thank you all for attending this meeting. You are welcome to leave, but don't forget what was mentioned today," Stacy said last minute.

While walking with Melissa, I saw Todd waiting for her in the lobby. She introduced me to him, and I got this weird vibe from him that I couldn't shake off. He had this demeanor like he was better than everyone. Something about him didn't sit right with my spirit. I just ignored it and said hello. He responded, and we had this awkward silence. The whole situation seemed forced, and I wanted no part of it. Melissa said that they were getting dinner and asked if I wanted to join.

I didn't feel like being a third wheel, so I politely declined. I was kind of feeling sad, despite me telling them no. Like would Melissa have asked me if he wasn't with her? I bet they were having a great time without me. Anyways, that's okay. I didn't go where I was not wanted. I could tell by her boyfriend's demeanor he wasn't happy for me to tag along. I walked back to the room, and immediately felt tired. I realized that I hadn't eaten in a while. Instead of asking Jeremy if he wanted dinner, I ordered Chinese take-out.

I decided to order four chicken wings and fried rice. Once I got my delivery, I immediately headed straight to my room. I figured I would watch *A Different World*. I was watching the episode where Jaleesa and Walter were planning on getting married. Whitley and Dwayne were decorating the main lobby of the dorm for their wedding. Dwayne asked Whitley what she looked for in a guy. She said he must be educated, enterprising, and ambitious.

He replied, "What if he's poor?"

Whitley said that kind of man was never poor. A while later, they kissed. I thought that was the most amazing part ever. I started to tear up because love was so beautiful, especially with the right person.

I eventually fell asleep. When I woke up, it was twelve in the afternoon. I didn't think I could sleep for that long. I saw that my roommate was laid up in the bed with her boyfriend. I immediately got uncomfortable because she didn't notify me that he would be spending the night. I wondered how long he was staying. I felt disrespected. I ended up getting ready for the day.

I checked my phone and saw I had a missed call from Veronica and a text message from Jeremy. I immediately called Veronica because this might be an emergency.

"Hey Veronica, I'm returning your call. Hope everything is alright with you."

"Hey Afua, I am going through a lot, and I just want someone to hear me out. My father is sick in the hospital. Can you believe he had a heart attack while we were at home? This came as a shock to everyone, because he's relatively healthy."

"I am so sorry, Veronica. I am here for you if you need to vent. Never think for a second you can't confide in me."

All this while I wished I was back in Brooklyn. I would've gone to her house and given her solace. This wasn't something you went through alone. She was crying hysterically on the phone; I tried to console her. "Veronica, your dad is a fighter. He will get through this and so will your family."

We sit on the phone and pray for what felt like twenty minutes.

When I got off the phone, I could tell that Veronica was in a better space mentally. I forgot that Jeremy sent me a text. He said how amazing it felt to have met me. My heart skipped a beat. I felt tense and nervous all at the same time.

He continued with, "I'm starting to like you and I wanted to know, can I take you on a date tonight?" I was overcome with excitement. I wanted to scream from the rooftops, but my roommate and her man were still sleeping and because I was in a dorm, I couldn't make too much noise. I couldn't believe he really liked me, but this was all so soon. I wondered if he was moving too fast. Only time would tell.

I accepted his date proposal. I was legit smiling so much. Could you tell I'm hype? I felt like I was on top of the world. I suspected he liked me, but to have my suspicions confirmed felt so good. I wanted to scream into my pillow, but I realized that would be rude. When I was happy or sad, I liked to listen to music. I grabbed my AirPods and proceeded to play my music. I stumbled across one of my favorites: "yes/no" by Banky W. It brought back memories of summer barbeques with my family at Prospect Park. I missed those times the most. Being around loved ones was the most essential part of my life; without them, I felt lost.

I wanted to tell Veronica, but she was going through a lot emotionally. So, I kept the excitement to myself. Before I knew it, Melissa and Todd were awake. Melissa said good afternoon while Todd just looked at his phone. He didn't even bother trying to make conversation with me. It was as if I didn't exist. I mean, not like he must.

"I'm going to watch a movie with Todd at the movie theaters. You want to come with?" Melissa asked.

"No thanks," I politely declined.

"Are you sure? It'll be a lot of fun," Melissa said.

"Yeah, I have plans later on."

Melissa scrunched her nose, and I could tell by her face she wanted to inquire, but she didn't. We stopped talking and I went back to listening to music. The whole time, I felt negative vibes from Todd. I couldn't pinpoint why I felt that way. Something about him didn't sit right with me. Even though I didn't know him I felt a bad vibe but maybe it would change.

My music playlist was incredible in my own opinion. I had different playlists for gospel, old school, and African music. I was jamming to my African playlist and daydreaming about the date with Jeremy. I wondered if he'd kiss me. I hadn't had my first kiss. All of this was new to me, and the more I thought, the more nervous I became. Why did I do this to myself? I got all worked up over nothing. I must believe that everything would go well. Omg, come to think of it, I didn't even know what I was going to wear. I looked in my closet and didn't see anything nice enough to wear. Then I remembered that I had a few dresses in my dresser that I could wear. I spotted my red off-the-shoulder dress. Bingo! *This is the one*, I say in my head.

I thought about the previous day and Jeremy's thoughtfulness towards his sister Naomi. I decided that his nickname would be Teddy for now. He was named after the stuffed animal he got for his sister. I thought that was a cute nickname. It was a perfect fit for him. I watched YouTube on my phone to pass the time. I watched girl advice videos on dating and what to expect. I was lost in all this, and I just wanted to brace myself for what would happen. Only you couldn't predict how a situation would be. Two hours passed by before Melissa and Todd decided to leave for the movies. Melissa said bye to me before they left. I expected that they would be out all day, which was good for me.

I sat in my dorm, having racing thoughts about the date going downhill. I didn't want to have a bad experience. I thought about the advice my parents gave me about being careful with guys. Every guy I've ever liked was too intimidated by me. Here I was with this guy, and he wasn't the least apprehensive about me. He liked me for me and that was the best thing ever. I continued watching YouTube for a few additional hours. Eventually, I grew extremely bored because I'd watched all my favorite YouTubers and there was nothing left to watch.

I figured I could start doing my makeup. I played my Afrobeats playlist. I sat at my desk and did my makeup flawlessly. I put that highlighter on my cheek bone and felt like a queen. I couldn't forget to put my lipstick on. I wore a brown liner with my nude lipstick and applied gloss over it. I was feeling myself, as people would say. I took a few pictures and put them on my Instagram story. I noticed that a few guys were sending me heart eyes. I rolled my eyes because in high school these guys wouldn't say anything to me. I got some likes on my story by a couple people, which elevated my self-esteem.

I felt so confident in myself, and nothing would bring me down. I got a text message from Jeremy, and he said that I could meet with him in an hour. Here I was, smiling again. This guy really made me happy, and to think I met him two days ago. I hadn't been this happy in a while. I suffered from depression from time to time. I wasn't clinically diagnosed, but I knew how my body responded to stress. When I got stressed out, it put me into a bout of depression. The weeks leading up to this weekend had been wonderful for me. Despite being away from home and my roommate troubles so far, I was loving it in college. I hoped I didn't speak too soon.

It was almost time to meet up with Jeremy, and I was growing anxious to see him. A while passed and I checked my phone, and it was time. I walked to the main lobby, and as usual, he was standing there. He wore a black button-down collared shirt and pants to match. He also had this chain with a cross on, which I thought was cute. As soon as he saw me, he said I looked stunning. I couldn't stop smiling. The front desk worker said that we looked amazing. I said thank you. The moment we shared felt like a fairytale. He leaned in for a hug, and this time he smelled like Bleu de Chanel. The only reason I knew what he smelled like was because I used to go into Macy's and smell perfume and cologne at the fragrance department.

I could tell he had good taste in cologne. We left the dorm and entered the parking lot. I saw that he drove a black Nissan Altima. The car was so beautiful. As the gentleman he was, Jeremy opened the door for me. The car looked amazing on the inside as well. He suggested that we go to Applebee's, and I agreed because I wasn't too familiar with restaurants here. He played Caribbean music. The song that came on was this '90s song that I couldn't remember the title for. It reminded me of the good old times when music made you experience something spiritual. You felt the aura of the music and it transcended you into a different space mentally. We were singing along with the lyrics and immediately, my spirit was elevated. Music could really put me in an amazing mood.

As we reached Applebee's, my appetite grew. I realized that I hadn't eaten all day. Finally, we arrived at the restaurant, and he opened the door. I thought about how chivalrous he was towards me. We were greeted by a lady and she seated us in a nice booth. A few minutes later, our server came and introduced himself as Trevor. He asked us what kind of drinks we wanted. I opted for blue raspberry lemonade while Jeremy got a dragon fruit lemonade.

The whole time I was thinking, *this can't be real.* I was like, *me out of all people to be on a date with a guy I have a crush on?* It was an incredible moment. He was asking me how I felt about the date. I said I was feeling good.

He replied, "I'm glad, because I was nervous you would reject me."

I was over the moon in excitement. I couldn't believe that Jeremy thought I would reject him. He really cared what I thought. My mind was racing, and I didn't know what to say. I just told him that I would never reject him. That he hadn't given me a reason to, like most guys I'd come across.

We placed our orders with the waiter. I ordered a classic bacon cheeseburger and Jeremy got a blackened Cajun salmon. We had a great conversation. As I said before, it was as if I knew him my whole life. We talked about our favorite shows and movies. We had the same morals and values. I learned that he was also practicing abstinence, which he said used to turn off girls in college. I was filled with joy because men like him were hard to come by. Later, we decided to share a blue-ribbon brownie. Our dessert was impeccable.

When it was time to pay for the bill, did you know this man decided to take the bill and pay for it? I even offered to split the bill and he simply said no. He was telling me that his mom and dad raised him to treat women right. I was completely shocked. I thought about how he was better than that guy Veronica had a date with. On our way out, I kept thinking how blessed I was to have met him. He was truly a godsend. We were in his car talking, and suddenly Jeremy leaned in and kissed me. It caught me completely off guard.

Oh my god, he really liked me. He told me that he was sorry if he came onto me too strongly. I told him that I wanted him to kiss me. This moment was so special. Jeremy also said that he really liked me and wanted to start dating. My face told it all: I was perplexed. How could he want me out of all people? This must be a dream I was having. *Somebody pinch me,* I thought. He asked me what I was thinking. I said I felt the same way.

He lit up with excitement and said, "I was hoping you felt the same way about me."

Jeremy drove back to our dorm. Before we got out of the car, I gave him a kiss on the cheek and thanked him for a wonderful night. We walked to the dorm and a different desk staff said we looked so good together. We both said thank you. Then looked at each other and smiled. He gave me a hug and we exchanged goodbyes. As I walked to my dorm room, the feeling of joy filled my heart. I entered my room, and no one was around. I began smiling so much that I lost track of time for a moment. I was in a daze. Overall, it was an amazing night.

I took off my makeup and headed into the bathroom to take a shower. I went back to my room and got ready for bed. Before I settled into bed, I needed to watch a movie. I decided to watch *Seventeen Again*. You know, the one with Tia and Tamera Mowry. I loved this movie. Especially the part when the grandparents forgave one another at the school dance. Love was sweet when it was with the right person. At that moment, I was thinking about Jeremy and me. I wanted us to end up officially dating and have a happy ever after together. I knew I was thinking far ahead but I was falling for this guy.

I really liked this movie. It showed that love was worth fighting for. Even when you've given up, there was someone that would show you otherwise. It didn't matter how long it took, sometimes love conquered all. I ended up falling asleep. Before I knew it, the time was around 10 am. Just as I was waking up from my rest, I saw that Melissa was alone in the bed, sleeping. I wondered what happened to Todd. Maybe he left. Rather than continue this thought, I got ready for the day. After I finished, I checked my phone and saw this beautiful text from Jeremy.

He said, "Thanks for spending the night with me at the restaurant, I really enjoyed myself. I'm hoping we can do this again."

I texted him back that I enjoyed myself and would like to hang out more. I soon realized that I hadn't spoken to my parents. They must be worried about me. If I didn't call them, they would figure something bad happened to me. They were also overprotective. Which was ironic that they allowed me to live three hours away from them.

I called my mom and she answered. "Are you okay? I thought something happened to you."

"Mom I'm okay, I just am getting adjusted to college life."

"Afua, you shouldn't forget about your family, because at the end of the day, we're all you have, and we'll be there for you no matter what. Wote ase? (Do you understand?)"

I knew that family would always be there. When my mom said this, I kind of felt bad for not calling them.

"Mom, I'm sorry for not calling you. I've been preoccupied by life and completely forgot. I agree with you that I should call more often."

"I understand, my daughter, but always remember family comes first."

They should also know I was in college and life happened. I needed them to understand I couldn't always call them each day.

After I got off the phone with my mom, I decided to call Veronica and see how things were going with her dad. "Hey, Veronica, how's your dad doing?"

"By God's grace, everything is fine with him. He's on a strict diet. He must eat heart-friendly foods, which he's not so happy about, but he'll be okay. I'm just happy he's alive. You never know how essential family is until you have a family emergency."

"So, sis, how are things going at college?" Veronica continued.

"Well, things have been great thus far. I met some new people, and Jeremy asked me out on a date."

"See, I told you he liked you." She was overwhelmed with excitement.

"Jeremy was a real gentleman towards me. We kissed, and it felt magical. The feelings were mutual between us."

"I can't believe this is happening for you. You really met an amazing guy, which is hard to come by. You struck gold, my friend."

"I guess I did," I said. The thought of reminiscing about last night made me so happy. I really had a good first date and I hoped to have many more.

. . .

Veronica and I talked about other things happening in our life. We had so much to catch up on.

"What TV shows have you been watching, Afua?"

"I don't know I've kind of stuck to my old sitcoms, like *A Different World*. However, I have been watching *The Chi*."

"Oooh, *The Chi* is a good show, I heard. Isn't it about people living in Chicago and all the issues going on there?"

"Yes, it has so much drama but it's very interesting. I can't stop myself from binge watching it," I add.

"Girl, me too. I've been watching my comfort shows like *This is Us* and *New Amsterdam*."

After my phone call, I decided to order lunch because I still didn't have my ID. I decided to get a bacon cheeseburger calzone and onion rings from this place called Pizza King. It was pricey, but well worth the money. I sat there watching *The Chi*.

It was an urban kind of show. There were real life struggles that some of the characters went through, such as battling homelessness and avoiding crime.

After a while, I checked the classes that I would have for the semester. I remembered registering for classes over the summer. I had some guidance on what classes to take from my advisor. I was enrolled in Psychology 101, English 101, Sign Language and Math 101. I was most excited about Psychology and Sign Language. Sign Language especially, because I always wanted to learn ever since I saw the movie *Sound and Fury*. It's about a deaf family and their daughter wanting to get a cochlear implant. The parents were against it, but the grandparents thought it was a good idea. I was really excited to learn ASL.

Reality Sets In

LIFE WAS ABOUT TO GET HECTIC FOR ME. I FINISHED THE FIRST THREE WEEKS of college. The first week was syllabus week, so it wasn't too bad. I felt like if I stay organized, I'd have a good semester. I finally got my ID from the student services center. They took my picture, which didn't take long. It cost me nothing, since it was my first student ID. Guess what! I decided to get a job. I saw a posting for a desk attendant at the library. I immediately applied, knowing that positions would be limited. I got called back for an interview. They asked me about myself and my work experience. I thought I wouldn't get the job because I was nervous, but I did.

My job was basically to help students find books for research and other purposes. They also had DVDs and CDs that people could rent out. Professors had books that students who took their courses could borrow. I also refilled the printer paper and checked how many students were in the library. My favorite part of the job was that I could do homework there. I met amazing people on the job that I thought could become my friend. I met this girl named McKenzie and she was nice. We normally had the same shift. So far, it was the best job ever.

As far as me and Jeremy, things were going well. Despite our busy schedule he made time to see me. We tried to get lunch or dinner with each other. Sometimes we ate with his friends Gabriel and Alyssa. I enjoyed their company because they were funny and gave off good vibes. So far, we'd been on one other date, which was the movies. We watched *Enola Holmes* which was a good mystery movie. Jeremy loved mysteries and action movies. We had so much fun together. I guess you could say we were an item.

As for my roommate, we were okay until we started having issues. We completed the roommate agreement the first week of school. There were things that we agreed not to do. Well, she didn't keep to it. She would stay up at all hours of the night with the light on. Even though I told her I had a job and needed to catch up on sleep. That annoyed me so much. She got upset when I said no overnight guests without notifying each other first. It was common courtesy to let each other know things that involved our shared space. I introduced her to Jeremy before all of this. I could sense that she liked him, but I didn't have solid evidence. She was so happy to meet him and kept giving him compliments. *Sis, I see what you're trying to do.* I guess you could say I had that woman's intuition.

I was at the dining hall trying to get lunch when I spotted Stacy. "Afua! Would you like to have a seat next to me?" Stacy called out.

I accepted her offer and sat down beside her. "So, how's school going for you?"

"It's not too bad since it's just the beginning. I'm really excited for my sign language class."

Stacy smiled. "That's great! What are you learning right now?"

"We are learning how to create a name sign for ourselves. Normally in the deaf community, a member creates a nickname for you."

"Wow, that's very interesting! I never knew that," Stacy said. Talking about something I was passionate about always made me happy.

"Afua, have you started thinking about clubs you would like to join? You know it's important to be involved on campus. So that you can get to know more people and network."

"I have thought about it, but I have been kind of busy with work and keep forgetting."

"Well, I am inviting you to come to the Curly Hair Club. I think you would like it very much."

I had totally forgotten about clubs since the involvement fair hadn't happened yet.

"We talk about issues pertaining to natural hair in the workforce and school. We also teach people how to better take care of their hair and during the semester we have a hair show."

All of it sounded interesting to me. I agreed to attend one of the meetings.

"How are things going with your roommate?"

"Melissa and I aren't on good terms. Sometimes Melissa would be nice and other times I don't even know who she is. She has this attitude with me out of nowhere. She does things without being considerate of me."

"If you want, I can have a meeting with the two of you to resolve the issue."

"Perhaps in the future, but for now, I can handle it," I said confidently, in hopes that what I said was true.

"If you ever need anything, let me know. I'm here to help."

I appreciated it because she didn't have to look out for me. After our conversation, I left the dining hall to go back to my room. I entered the room to find Melissa crying on the phone. I assumed it was about Todd because he and Melissa were having relationship troubles lately. She didn't care that I was in the room. So, I just tried to mind my business but that didn't work.

She kept saying, "How can you say mean things to me and think I won't react? You always belittle me and put me down. What's so wrong with showing me respect? I am a human being with feelings and emotions. Did you ever consider what I'm going through?"

Melissa saying this confirmed my belief about him, which didn't help. That was the main reason I did not want to become too invested into their relationship.

When she got off the phone, she began crying again. I hated seeing people cry. It made me unhappy. I was an empath which meant I felt other people's pain.

"Melissa, are you okay?"

"Why do you care?" she said with an attitude and dismissed me like I was nothing.

At that moment, I could've told her off, but it wasn't in me to do that. "If you need me, I'll be here."

She just ignored me and continued to cry into her pillow. I had sympathy for people at times because I know if I were in that situation, I would want the same treatment. I just went back to learning how to sign the alphabet.

The sign alphabet wasn't too bad for me to learn. Although some of the letters were difficult for me to remember. I ended up watching a YouTube video because the book was hard to follow. I was afraid that if I didn't study often, I'd fail. This stemmed from when I was younger, my parents always told me to be the best. They taught me that if I wasn't getting A's in school, I was failing. They would say, "Look at all the kids in third world countries that want to learn but can't. You have every chance to learn, you must seize the opportunity."

Some of my teachers would praise me for being smart which gave other people a reason to dislike me. I eventually learned to ignore them. Sometimes I thought that I was a failure if I didn't get an A on every assignment. It's been instilled in me to always be the best. Especially since I was the oldest, I must be an example for my other siblings.

I had to work extra hard, so I could prove to myself and others that anything was possible and within your reach if you worked hard enough. It's not only me that will be affected, but also my family. There's an African proverb that says, "You are beautiful; But learn to work, for you cannot eat your beauty." This meant that you must have other things going for yourself than just a pretty face. You must work hard for what you want in life because nothing gets handed to anyone. My family was a constant reminder of why I couldn't give up, and believe me, I tried. As I did my assignment, I prayed for God to give me guidance.

My family was very religious. We went to church almost every Sunday. When I was young, I was brought up in the church of Pentecost. I remember there being Bible competitions to see who knew all the books of the Bible. We used to have children's and youth day where people would recite memory verses, preach, dance, etc. I always cherished those times. I met amazing friends, such as Josephine (Josie for short) and Charlotte. We still communicated, but I hadn't heard from them in a while. After I finished studying, I'd reach out to them in the group chat.

I started to get the hang of the sign alphabet and even started to learn how to say my name. I thought how the deaf community communicated with one another was cool. I finished studying and then remembered to text Josephine and Charlotte.

ME:

Hey how's everyone been?

CHARLOTTE:

OMG hey!

JOSIE:

It's been forever since we last chatted.

ME:

Sis tell me about it.

CHARLOTTE:

How's life going in college?

ME:

I'm meeting new people and adjusting to college coursework.

JOSIE:

That's good to know. We are praying for you.
I have a question.

ME:

Ask away Josie

JOSIE:

So, sis, have you met anyone special these days?

ME:

You did not waste anytime in asking. LOL.
Well if you must know yes I have started dating someone.

CHARLOTTE:

Really? Wow I'm so happy for you.

JOSIE:

Me too. Our little girl has grown wings.
Tell us more about him.

ME:

I know I'm the baby of the group. You both are two years older than me. Anyways his name is Jeremy and he's a sophomore at my school. He's a gentleman and I really like him. We've been on dates but aren't officially boyfriend and girlfriend yet.

CHARLOTTE:

That sounds wonderful. But remember to pray about the situation and him to know if he's a suitable partner.

JOSIE:

I totally agree with Charlotte. I'm happy for you but make sure you pray about it. Some of these men be out of control out here. If you get what I mean.

ME:

I get what you both mean and I will pray about it. I know prayer is an integral part of our walk as Christians. Hopefully he makes me his girlfriend soon.

JOSIE:

He will at the right time don't rush a relationship with any man. Make sure you and him align first in values and morals. Always remember he should be lucky to have you.

CHARLOTTE:

Exactly. You stole the words right out of my mouth lol.

ME:

I totally agree. It's just it's my first dating experience. He has me feeling happy and loved. I hope the feelings are mutual.

CHARLOTTE:

My sista you better pray about it lol. I'm sure the feelings are mutual and if not you will know.

JOSIE:

I totally agree with Charlotte. Home girl knows what she's talking about. We have dated before, and we know that it's important to pray and take your time knowing him. Don't rush. God's got you so give all your worries to him. We also got your back if this boy wants to play games lol.

CHARLOTTE:

Thanks I try Afua we always got your back.

ME:

Thanks Girls I really appreciate you both. This is a reminder to keep God first in everything I do. TTYL

JOSIE:

No problem TTYL

CHARLOTTE:

TTYL XOXO

I got a knock on my door, and I answered it to see Jeremy. Wow, and to think I was just talking about him to my friends. He gave me a big hug. Jeremy always smelled good, which was a turn-on for me. As usual, he smelled like One Million cologne. He asked me if I wanted to grab McDonalds with him. I said yes because anything was better than being with Melissa. We walked to his car, and he drove us to get fast food. We both got a quarter pounder with bacon and cheese meal. He got Sprite while I got a McFlurry. No surprise, he paid for it all despite my attempt to pay.

As we drove back to the dorm, Jeremy talked a lot about how he was lucky to have met me. I noticed that when he's nervous, he'll say, "Wow, that's crazy," at the end of every sentence. I knew that he was a bit tense in telling me how he felt. He said most people on campus didn't try to get to know him. They just tried to use him. I told Jeremy that I would never want to take advantage of him. I cared about him too much to do that. This was the first time he'd ever said something like this to me. I felt honored that he even thought of me in that way. He told me that he had a date planned for us on Saturday. It was a surprise I wouldn't know until the day of.

Jeremy and I returned to the dorm and decided to eat in the main lounge. I noticed that nobody was in there yet. We just sat and talked about our day. "How was your day, Jeremy?"

"My boss had me dealing with money order receipts from students who decided to study abroad. The process isn't easy, but if I could, I'd study in another country."

"Oh, really? Where would you like to study?" "Maybe the United Kingdom or somewhere like Australia," Jeremy said.

"I'm curious, why those places?"

"I love the atmosphere over there and their accents are unique."

"I think that is so cool, Jeremy. If I had the opportunity, I'd go back to Ghana."

"I'll ask you the same question. Why would you love to study in Ghana?"

"It's a vibe over there. The people are so kind, and the rich cultures makes anyone want to stay."

"That's wassup, I think those are great reasons to go, Afua. I love your name, how did your parents come up with the name?"

"In one of the Ghanaian cultures known as Akan, children are named after the day that they were born. I was born on January 16th, 2004, which is a Friday, so my name is Afua. It's special to me because it's a representation of my heritage."

"Wow that's really interesting, I didn't know that!" Jeremy exclaimed.

"When is your birthday?" I asked him.

"My birthday is April 19th, 2003."

I Googled what day he was born, and it said Saturday.

"That means your name would be Kwame."

He became overjoyed. "My name is Kwame aye."

I laughed because it was funny, the way he said it.

I returned to my room after my time with Jeremy. I debated on what other names I should call him. I liked having pet names for him. I thought it was cute even though people might find it annoying. It was always a good time with him. He gave me this good feeling that I'd never felt. I prayed that I wasn't wrong about him. I entered my dorm and Melissa was still looking sad, but no longer crying, which was a good sign. I didn't say anything because I tried to help, and she rejected my kindness. I thought about the fact that I was over here with a nice guy while she was dealing with trash. I wanted to give her some advice, but I realized that I'd be overstepping my boundaries. If I could talk to her, I'd tell her to cut her losses with that guy. He was bringing her down spiritually and that wasn't good. I just went to bed and scrolled through Instagram.

The next day, I had an early shift at work because I didn't have class in the mornings on Tuesday and Thursdays. I saw my friend McKenzie and greeted her. She happened to be my closest friend at work. We talked about school and how things were going thus far. We were both freshman and loved reading. She kept trying to get me to read the book *You are a Badass* by Jen Sincero. She claimed that it was a great book about living your best life regardless of what others think. I thought about reading the book because I struggled with my confidence and thinking about people's perception of me. I suggested that she read *Daring Greatly* by Brené Brown. It talked about vulnerability and how to deal with it. That it was okay to be vulnerable because it developed meaningful connections with others.

An hour passed by at work and a student came by asking for help with her assignment. She told me her name was Blake and I thought,

That's a unique name. She was doing a history paper on a historical leader. She ended up choosing Nelson Mandela, but she was panicking because her paper was due this week. I tried to tell her to calm down. She told me that she was a freshman and that it was important she do well this semester. We both bonded over the fact that we were freshmen. I told her that I was here to help. Blake told me that she was struggling in this class. I said that it was a good thing she came to the library because we'd help her get started on that paper. I told her that she would do alright if she changed her mindset. I helped her find some articles and two books about him. She thanked me and went into the library to start her assignment.

I had a feeling of accomplishment helping Blake with her assignment. I loved helping people in any way I could. What I loved most about this job was that I could help people with their research papers. I ended up having to do rounds to see the population of people at the library. Sometimes we were full, and other times, like now, it was pretty dead. I saw Blake, who introduced me to her friends. She told them how I helped her with research for her paper. She said I was a life saver, which made me happy. I told her thank you and good luck. I didn't want to distract her by talking so much since she needed to focus on her assignment. I realized that people at my job were so nice. It brought me joy to be here during my shifts.

Another hour passed by, and I saw my roommate. She gave me a look when I said hi to her, and proceeded to walk past without saying anything. That was when I realized she didn't like me.

McKenzie said, "What was that all about?"

I told McKenzie that I had no idea why she treated me like that. She had mood swings. One moment she was happy and wanted to talk to me, and other times were like this.

McKenzie said, "That's not right for her to be angry with you all the time. Especially since you haven't done anything but be nice to her. If you ever get tired of the treatment, I suggest you move out and find another roommate or request a single."

I thought about that idea but I wasn't sure if I wanted to move all my things across campus. I liked my RA and wanted to stay. I told McKenzie that I'd think about it. She told me that she also had issues with her roommate because she was messy.

That was very inconsiderate of her, which she agreed with. It was difficult having roommates. Especially ones that the school assigned. I thought those videos I watched were exaggerated, but now I knew the truth. After this year, I could pick my own roommate. Maybe McKenzie and I could room together. I couldn't wait until the end of my sophomore year to officially move off campus. It would be nice if I found decent roommates. My shift was over, and McKenzie asked me if I wanted to go to Walmart with her. I said yes because I had nothing planned for the rest of the day.

We decided to wait for the shuttle bus to come in front of the college center. The college center was a building where you could get food, buy tickets for events, and had meetings for clubs. Events take place there too. We waited fifteen minutes before the shuttle came and then we got inside. We arrived at Walmart and began shopping. I needed a few things, such as snacks and personal care items. McKenzie needed to buy some personal care items as well.

I had a shopping addiction. If I wasn't careful, I could spend 100 to 200 dollars easily in a single shopping trip. I was a college student, I couldn't afford to spend money recklessly. I told McKenzie to tell me if I bought too many things. We talked about getting involved on campus. I kept forgetting to attend the Curly Hair Club and ASO. I bet I'd enjoy myself more if I attended these organizations. Plus, I was invited to one of the clubs by Stacy. I knew she expected me to come. I thought, *I'll make time to go next week.* McKenzie said that she was interested in the Anime club. I didn't know she was interested in that. She said that her boyfriend introduced her to Sailor Moon and Yu Yu Hakusho. After that, she'd been hooked ever since.

We talked about our dating life. McKenzie told me about her boyfriend Ezra. He went to New Paltz and was studying early childhood education with an environmental science minor.

"Ezra has plans on becoming a teacher one day. I met him in junior year of high school, and we've been together for almost two years. He respects and treats me right. If he didn't, I wouldn't waste any time doing long-distance because it gets difficult. Sometimes you just want that close proximity to your significant other."

"I get what you mean, McKenzie, dating takes work and effort."

"Exactly! Both partners have to want to make the relationship work. Ezra is trying to come and see me soon when he's not too busy. How did you and Jeremy meet?"

"Well, me and Jeremy met when I was walking towards the dorm we both live at. I accidentally bumped into him, and the rest is history. We've kind of been inseparable ever since."

"Wow! I'm amazed at the way you two hit it off after that encounter. Who initiated the dating process?"

"It was Jeremy, he texted me one day and asked to go on a date. I agreed and that's when we started dating shortly after."

"Be careful, normally upperclassmen try to take advantage of freshmen because they are new and impressionable. Some guys try to have their way with girls sexually. I am only talking out of experience, being at school thus far."

"McKenzie, you are right, because I heard the same thing from watching YouTube."

McKenzie is an EOP student. EOP stands for the Educational Opportunity Program. It helped students that were struggling academically and financially gain admission to college. They had to stay at the school during the summer for about six weeks, doing course work and other activities.

"EOP is the best. It's like a close-knit family of people that support and nurture you." I saw how the guys used to act towards girls they liked. "You should pay attention to Jeremy's actions and see if he's worthy of being your boyfriend. Write down a list of some characteristics you like about him and see if they outweigh the bad. Then you'll have your answer about him."

I took heed to the advice because I knew she was only speaking from experience. She had good intentions in telling me this.

We walked around for what felt like an hour. I ended up getting bottles of water, chips, Pop Tarts, banana nut muffins, body wash, hair products and some toiletries. McKenzie got what she needed, which was feminine hygiene products. We also bought Subway because we both hadn't eaten. I got a chicken and bacon ranch sandwich, but instead of ranch, I used Chipotle Mayo. I also got white chocolate macadamia nut cookies. McKenzie got an Italian BMT which consisted of beef salami, pepperoni, and chicken ham. She also got chocolate chip cookies. I spent a little under 100 dollars, which wasn't bad. I decided that my stuff was too much to carry, so I called an Uber. McKenzie decided to share one with me, because waiting for the shuttle would take a long time. The Uber came a few minutes later and drove us back to campus. As we were driving, I heard the chorus of that '90s song Jeremy and I were listening to a while back. I immediately got to thinking about him. That was when I realized I was falling for him more than I thought.

We approached my dorm, and the driver helped me take my things out. I waved bye to McKenzie before heading back inside.

I went into my room and put my stuff away. I noticed that Melissa wasn't around, which was nice. I ate my sandwich while watching *Kenan and Kel*. I loved '90s TV shows. They were the golden era of TV shows, especially for black people. Once I finished, I started thinking about what McKenzie said about writing a list. I decided at that moment I would grab a book and write down things I liked and disliked about Jeremy. I wrote down Teddy on the top of the page, because that was my nickname for him. I wrote in one column things I liked, and in the other, things I disliked. The things I liked about him was that he was chivalrous, good with money, intelligent, tall, family oriented and humble. The list got so long that when I got to dislikes, I barely had any. The only dislike was that he was always busy, but all his good qualities made up for it. That was when it hit me that he was a guy I saw myself dating long term. I still had no idea where he was taking me for our next date. That man was very romantic, so I knew it was going to be someplace good.

I spent the rest of the night catching up on my favorite shows. It was a great night being alone. Sometimes it was important to have alone time. It's a part of self-care. So, whenever my roommate wasn't around, I took advantage. I ended up falling asleep and what happened next threw me for a loop. I had a dream that Jeremy was helping me take down my braids. I never thought that guys would do that since it was a tedious process. I appreciated him doing it with me, because he didn't have to. As he took down my hair, he said how beautiful it was and that I should wear my hair out more. I was so happy that he loved my natural beauty. My family was there, which was odd. They all were cool with him being there. It was as if he was one of the family. My parents didn't give me any hints that they disliked him. The dream ended with him just laughing and joking around with my family. I woke up in such a good mood. I was smiling, but deep down inside I wished the dream had continued.

The dream might have been a sign that Jeremy was a good guy and wouldn't hurt me. Maybe he'd ask me soon to be his girlfriend. I hoped he did, because if not, then it would confirm my doubts that I was wasting my time. I prayed about this situation all the time. I wanted God to give me guidance in what to do next. If he was the right one for me, may his actions speak for itself. I was sure he wouldn't treat me badly because that wasn't in his nature. Here I was, overthinking again. Why couldn't I let things flow? My parents always taught me to not settle for less than what I deserved. Self-worth was instilled in me since I was young. I might not always have the best self-esteem, but I knew I was worthy of love. They taught me to date with purpose. That purpose was a long-term relationship that ended in marriage. I wasn't thinking that far ahead, but at least I'd like to be in a serious relationship. Anyways, enough of me thinking about that. *Let's get ready,* I told myself.

After I got ready, I decided to call my parents because I hadn't heard from them in a while. I FaceTimed my mom and she told me that it was nice to hear from me.

"Afua, how's school going?"

"So far, it's going well. I have a job now."

"Make sure you make time for school. It's very important for you to prioritize your education above all else."

"Mommy, I know how important school is." Then she proceeded to ask me about my dating life again. "Remember the nice guy that I was telling you about? Well, he lives in my dorm. He's smart and driven. We have the same mindset and values. He took me out on a date and we have been dating ever since."

"Wow, can we meet him?"

"We haven't made it official yet, but when we do, I'll be glad to introduce him." One thing about my mom, she will ask intrusive questions. She knew that I was an open book with her. I tried not to hide things from my parents.

"I think you should really get to know him to see his character. Most relationships in college don't work out. You must not get lost in love that you forget about yourself."

"I agree with you." I valued my mom's advice because it always came from the heart.

Moments later, I asked my mom about my dad, and she said he wasn't around. "Your dad went to work and should be back in a few hours." My dad was an IT specialist. He worked a lot of hours sometimes. I didn't always get a chance to speak to him often. "How are you adjusting to school life?"

"I'm loving my sign language class."

"What are you learning in class and what made you choose sign language over other languages?"

"I am learning how to sign my name and the alphabet. Also, how to sign sentences. Sign language is very unique and expressive in nature."

"How's things going with your roommate?"

"We aren't the best of friends. We are practically strangers living together."

"I advise you to not mind your roommate and make friends with people that want to see you succeed. Don't waste your time on people that won't matter to you in the next year. As long as you have a clean heart, it doesn't matter what the enemy tries to throw your way. It will not work."

My mom is dropping gems and I'm loving it.

"I pray for you to excel in whatever you do at school. For you to be surrounded by loving people who care about you. I pray that you will overcome any obstacle that comes your way and handle it with grace. May God protect your coming and going. In Jesus' name I pray, amen. Have a good rest of your day, my love."

"Talk to you later, Mom." I enjoyed my mother's prayers because she always looked out for my best interest. When she prayed, suddenly the very thing I was worried about went away. I could think clearly and see things for what they are.

I got up and decided that I was going to have a great day. I didn't know where this energy came from, but I was here for it. I was in such a good mood that I didn't even pay mind to Melissa giving me dirty looks. I ended up going to the library to get some work done. I saw some of my coworkers and said hello to them. I sat in one of the study carrels so I could focus on my work. I worked on my math assignment. I struggled in math. If I continued to struggle in this course, I would utilize the learning center and book a tutoring session. I had never been good at that subject. I preferred English over math because it wasn't as complicated.

While I was in the library, I saw Alyssa. We waved at one another. She came over and we talked about our course work. I told her how the struggle is real. "Math is the only class that's giving me a headache."

"I feel you on that one. That's why I chose my major, because it involves less math." Alyssa was an English major with a creative writing minor. She had plans to become an author in the future. We talked about other things and then she dropped a bombshell on me. "I just want to let you know that Jeremy really cares about you. You're the first girl on campus that didn't take advantage of his kindness."

She saw me smiling and Alyssa said, "I hope that made your day."

It most certainly did, because I was having my doubts. Alyssa would never lie to me. She was his friend which meant she knew him better than I did. I wondered if this was the sign I'd been looking for. The first sign was the dream and now this. I was filled with joy and I couldn't contain myself.

Alyssa left to go to work and wished me good luck with my assignment. I stayed in the library for another two hours doing homework. I realized that I didn't get anything to eat so I headed to The Circle, which was a place that had different kinds of food to take out. I decided to get stir fry. I got chicken, broccoli, and carrots. I also got a Brisk raspberry iced tea and a chocolate chip cookie. I paid for my food and then headed to my dorm with headphones on while listening to music. I entered my room and put my stuff down. I changed into my pajamas and then I started eating my food. At that moment I just thought about my life and how blessed I felt. It was a good feeling to be in college and not have to stress about how I'd repay my loans. God really looked out for me always.

My phone rang and it was Veronica.

"Hey girl, I just wanted to let you know that things are going good with my dad. He is doing well and making a full recovery."

"We thank God, because I thought something was wrong. So how's school going, Veronica?"

"Girl, school is alright, but I can tell it's going to become difficult as time progresses."

"I agree with you, sis."

"On another note, I have seen a few people from our school at college."

"Oh really? That must be nice." I was one of the small bunch that decided to go away for school. Most people stayed in NYC because of financial constraints. I always knew that I wouldn't stay in my comfort zone which was Brooklyn. I had to see what else was out there in the world.

"Afua, what about you? How's college going?"

"Veronica, so far, I love the school environment."

"Maybe it is because of a little someone."

"Ha-Ha-Ha, very funny. It might be true, but I've met some amazing people that have made my time great."

"So how's Jeremy doing?"

"Jeremy is good and his friend Alyssa said he really likes me. That he's never felt this way about anyone in a while."

"Wow, wow, wow, I'm completely shocked that other people know how he feels about you. It's a good thing that he tells his friends about you. I'll say this to you once: it's only a matter of time before he makes things official."

"Those words of yours is making me filled with joy."

Veronica and I talk for a long time and then we hung up because it was getting late. I ended up falling asleep as usual, and before I knew it, it was time to get ready for work. I noticed that it was very quiet in my dorm. I guessed it was because people hadn't gotten up yet. My roommate was gone. I assume she left for class. I tried not to keep up with what she was doing, but I found it odd she was up that early. I saw her before I went to sleep last night. Anyways, time to hurry up before I became late. I always prided myself on getting to work on time.

At work, it was getting busy and this time I was with other people instead of McKenzie. They put her to work on the main level while I worked on the third floor. The third level was normally for people that wanted to get work done. There was an extreme quiet section for people who need complete silence. It got intense over there and people looked at you strange if you talked. It was also for newspaper archives and older historical material. This floor was the perfect opportunity to work on my sign language. I was trying to learn how to come up with sentences, but I needed to learn the fundamentals first. I spotted Blake and she came over to my desk. She said she was doing better mentally. She also finished her paper and got a good grade on it. I was so happy to see her again because I was wondering how the assignment went. She asked me what I was doing, and I told her I was practicing my sign language.

We got into a conversation about the rules in sign language. There were some elements unique to signing such as handshape, palm orientation, movement, location, and expressions. After our conversation, Blake told me that she was headed to class. I made my rounds through the third floor and refilled the printer paper. My shift felt like it was taking forever and I slowly became sleepy. It was to be expected since I didn't get good sleep last night. I didn't know what it was. I just had a hard time staying asleep. It didn't help that Melissa was up watching her show on Netflix. Two hours passed and it was time for me to leave. I went to The Circle again because I couldn't be bothered to go to the dining hall. I ended up getting a pepperoni pizza and a lemonade. I still had the cookie from last night, which I might eat later.

I headed to my dorm room. Once I was at my dorm, I got a text from an unknown number, and it just said, "Hey."

I texted back, "Sorry, who is this?"

The person texted back and said, "It's your cousin Akosua and I wanted to check up on you."

I remembered her from when I was young, but we hadn't talked in some years. I wondered what she wanted.

AKOSUA:

How's school going?

ME:

School is fine.

AKOSUA:

That is good. You should make your parents proud in college and avoid sororities.

ME:

Thank you for the advice. I will not let my parents down nor involve myself in any sororities.

AKOSUA:

Have a good day. You can text me whenever.

ME:

Same to you

That encounter was awkward; good thing I didn't disclose anything to her. One thing about my cousin: she'd spread your business to the whole family. Before you knew it, people would begin talking about me and saying I was behaving wild. She liked konkonsa (gossiping) too much. I was confused about the sorority thing because I never mentioned I wanted to pledge. I recalled thinking about it, but ever since I heard about hazing and my church's discussion about denouncing Greek life, it turned me off from joining. I proceeded to watch a movie. Netflix had a bunch of African movies that I'd grown to love. I spent the rest of the day watching movies.

Four

Love

Today was the day I went on my surprise date. I didn't know what was in store for me today, but I was pumped. I was still in shock that I was dating because all my life I heard no boyfriend until eighteen. It was ingrained in my head that I should be careful of men. That they only had one intention. My parents would say if you came home pregnant, life would never be the same. You would struggle and that freedom you once had was out the window. They also threatened to send me to a boarding school in Ghana. Hearing those words used to scare me away from guys. It didn't help that most of them would ignore me. Over time I grew to love being ignored because it made me focus on school. I made huge accomplishments in my life and for that I was thankful. I decided to get ready for the day.

Once I was finished, I hopped into my bed and began eating Pop

Tarts. I was trying to save my appetite for my date tonight. I knew myself, if I ate too much, I might not have an appetite later. As usual, I watched YouTube videos and enjoyed my time. I got a text from Jeremy.

JEREMY:

Are you ready for tonight?

ME:

So, you aren't going to give me a hint as to what's going to happen?

JEREMY:

No because it will spoil the surprise. It's something I think you would love.

ME:

I hope it is incredibly fun because the suspense is bothering me.

JEREMY:

Do not worry, it'll be worth the wait. See you later.

ME:

See you 🤍

Most people who knew me understood that I was very impatient and I didn't do well with surprises. I wanted to know right then and there because I had weird reactions to things. I didn't press the issue further because anything was better than staying in my dorm all day.

Time passed and boredom struck. I was going to watch more African movies. I was watching my favorite movie, *Passion of the Soul*. It was about two lovers that couldn't be together because the girl's father disapproved. She got pregnant by this man, but the father had already arranged a marriage between her and another man. It's a sad story and the female main character, played by Jackie Appiah, ended up giving birth to a girl. Then the father lied to her and made her believe something happened to the child. The whole time, the father gave the baby to the biological father and told him to stay away for good. I assumed he gave him some hush money, but I couldn't remember. The movie had some funny elements to it as well. The movie showed that wickedness would never prevail. The father thought he was doing good by keeping his daughter away from her true love and her daughter. It's a timeless movie I could watch repeatedly.

As the time approached, I grew anxious about what would happen on our date. So many thoughts were running through my head. I was asking myself if all the signs that I experienced meant anything. *Girl, get out of your own head*, I told myself. I searched for something to wear tonight. I checked my dresser and remembered I had a nude dress I could wear. It had a square neckline, ruffled sleeves, and flared out. It's such a perfect date night outfit. I was going to wear gold jewelry, a black bag, and shoes with gold hardware. My hair was in box braids which was convenient for me. I lived for protective styles because it made life easier. I didn't have to think about my hair for a while. I decided I'd wear my hair in a side part. Now that I got that out the way, I wondered how I'd do my makeup. I thought I'd go for a natural glam with some false lashes.

I would look so good tonight. My hope was that he liked my outfit and complimented me. I wondered what he was going to wear. Anyways, Melissa was in the room. She saw me getting my outfit together and asked me where I was going. I rolled my eyes because she wasn't asking because she cared; she was trying to be nosy. I didn't feel like explaining my love life to someone that's not even my friend.

She said, "I'm assuming you're going out with that guy Jeremy. Well, if I were you, I'd be very careful. These guys are not to be trusted, and sooner or later he'll show his true colors." She continued, "Upperclassmen only go out with freshmen because no one in their year wants them."

I took her advice with a grain of salt because she was just projecting her insecurities onto me and I ain't having it. She could keep her advice to herself.

I asked her, "What makes you so sure he'll treat me like that?"

She didn't say anything for a minute, then said she had experience with men doing those things to her. It's always good in the beginning. "You know that Todd and I broke up? He got caught going on a date with my childhood friend. I only found out because my family friend Millie told me. She caught them at the movies. You know what his response was? He said I was away at school, and he felt lonely. I wasn't giving him the attention he needed. He said long distance was taking a toll on him. You think this man likes you now, but wait until another girl comes along, he'll forget all about you."

I looked at her, puzzled because I didn't understand where all this was coming from. Sure, she was cheated on, but she had no right to project her insecurities onto me.

I just said, "Well, thank you for the advice, but I don't think that'll be my story."

That's when she said, "Sooner or later, you'll see."

That conversation just put me in a bad mood. What she said put insecurities into my head. *Maybe she's right, what if he's trying to use me?* So many thoughts were running through my mind. *Why would Alyssa tell me that I'm the best girl he's ever met?* Melissa got me out here doubting that Jeremy likes me. Times like this I wished I had my friend Veronica by my side. She would've told Miss Thang off. I decided that I would listen to music to get my mind into a better place. I was going to have a wonderful night, and no one was going to tear me down. Just because men hurt Melissa didn't mean all men were the same. I put on my Afrobeats playlist because it's upbeat. I listened to music and instantly my spirit elevated.

Time passed and I figured that I would start doing my makeup. I really outdid myself, because my makeup looked so amazing. I was shocked and lost for words. I applied my lip gloss and my look was complete. I started taking selfies as usual and posted them on Instagram. People were loving the pictures and it immediately made me happy. I got over one hundred likes, which was a shock to me since I didn't follow many people. I saw under the comments that Jeremy wrote, *you are looking so gorgeous, can't wait to see you tonight.* I am so hype right now it's not even funny. I couldn't believe he wrote that under my post cause now people would know who I was dating. I was a very private person. I didn't like for people to know things unless I made the announcement. Anyways, I just let it go. Who cared what people thought; their opinions didn't matter.

After two hours it was time for me to get dressed and meet Jeremy, aka Teddy. I put on my clothes and looked into the mirror. I started smiling because I looked stunning. I texted Jeremy that I was coming, and he said he'd be waiting at the main lobby by the front desk. I stepped outside and walked towards the lobby. When I saw him, he was wearing a black shirt with white pinstripes going down and beige cargo pants. He has a gold chain on and white Air Force Ones. Of course, he looked good. He also had a fresh haircut which, if you knew me, I loved. He saw me and he was lost for words.

He said, "You look absolutely beautiful."

As always, the desk staff complimented us, which brought a warm feeling. He gave me a hug and I was over the moon. He smelled so good; I couldn't control myself.

We walked to his car, and I got all giddy. Whatever we were doing tonight, it must be fun. He held open the door for me. I entered his car, and it looked immaculate and smelled so good. I could tell he cleaned it to perfection.

"I'm excited to finally go on a date with you, I miss you, Afua."

"I know, we legit haven't seen one another in days. You're always so busy, but I respect that. It shows that you're ambitious."

"Yeah, I know I've been busy for a while."

"I miss you so much. At this moment I feel so grateful to have you in my life."

Jeremy smiled. "Afua, I'm happy to have you in my life." He drove me to this place called Painting with a Twist that had intricate colors outside. "We're here."

"Wow, you outdid yourself. I've always wanted to do a paint and sip when I was in Brooklyn, but it never happened."

"I was hoping you would like it." We walked in and were greeted by the host, Henry. He escorted us to our seats. Since we were under-age, he gave us soda to drink.

It was time for us to find out what we're painting. It's by the famous artist Vincent Van Gogh titled *Starry Night*. I'm not the best drawer or painter, but I was excited that I could keep my painting after I was done. The host began painting and we followed him.

"How did your week go?"

"It went well besides having issues with my roommate."

"Do not give her the energy she's looking for. She wants to get you riled up so you can fit the angry black woman narrative. Don't let her have the chance. You worked too hard to let someone take it away."

"She's just being bitter because things aren't going her way."

There's some truth to what he said. "You're right about that, she wants me to act a fool so I can get removed from the room and she can have a single. Melissa didn't know that I'm not the one to mess with."

"Enough talking about Melissa, how was your week?"

"I passed my organic chemistry exam. I studied so hard. It's good to know my hard work paid off. That's the highlight of my week besides being here with you."

"Aww, how sweet of you to say that. Immensely proud of you for doing well on your exam."

I noticed the calmness in his demeanor with me. The way he looked at me when he was excited about something he's passionate about.

"Also, work is getting hectic because more students are studying abroad."

"Really? Studying abroad is everyone's dream at the moment."

"Tell me about it."

As we copy the host it became apparent that I was no artist. "Jeremy, yours looks ten times better than mine." He just laughed. "I've been drawing for quite some time. I used to be a part of an art club growing up until I reached high school. We used to paint canvases and display them around the school. So, you can say I'm good at painting."

"Why am I now finding out about this? I feel like I learn something new about you every time."

We finished painting and I looked at mine, amazed 'cause I created something decent. The colors and the beautiful sky I drew made being here worthwhile. We stuck around a few to wait for our paintings to dry.

"I'm happy that I get to be here with you." He just smiled and my heart melted. All I could think was, *Am I falling in love?*

After our painting dried, we decided to leave. It was a great experience, and I didn't even know this place existed.

"Hey, do you want to go to Dave and Busters to eat?"

"Yes, I'm hungry, plus anything is better than going back to my dorm."

"It was fun painting. What a stress reliever. Thank you for taking me out."

He placed his hand on my thigh. "You are the best girl I have ever met. You know that I knew from the moment we met that you were special."

We ended up in the parking lot of Dave and Busters, but we had yet to enter.

He then said something that I'd been waiting for all along. Jeremy looked me in my eyes with love and care. "Will you be my girlfriend?"

Instantly I melted. I said yes and began crying. I didn't know I would get this emotional over someone expressing their love for me. It was all foreign to me. This was a whole new world to me. I was finally his girlfriend and I didn't know how to act.

We kissed and it was amazing. It felt like sparks flew. "I can't believe you asked me to be your girlfriend."

He said, "I always knew I would ask you, but didn't know how or when."

My mom always said a man knew what his intentions would be with you from the very start, so don't get surprised by his actions because he was telling you all along who he truly was.

Jeremy did something next that made me love him more. He said, "Medɔ wo."

I got immediately confused because at first, he wasn't saying it right. "What are you trying to say?"

"I'm trying to say *I love you* in Twi. I did some research and found out that 'Medɔ wo' is how you say I love you."

I taught him the proper pronunciation and then I started to cry even more. He didn't have to learn my language. But he did, and for that, he'd always have a piece of my heart.

A while later, we entered Dave and Busters. We were welcomed by the host Suzanne, and she escorted us to our seats. Then we were greeted by the server, Lizzie. She asked us what we would like to drink. I got a blue raspberry lemonade while Jeremy got a strawberry lemonade.

"What made you want to learn my language? I'm very pleased with your dedication."

"I am really interested in learning different languages and experiencing a vast amount of culture."

We got into the conversation about how many countries we've been to. "I've only been to Ghana."

"I have traveled to several countries including Trinidad, South Africa, Jamaica, and Dubai." He would like to travel to more places, but school was getting in the way. "I would also love to travel soon."

It was time for us to order food. I ordered a beast mode bacon burger and Jeremy gets a chicken avocado club. We decided to split cinnamon sugar churros for dessert. What could I say? I really loved burgers. If I was at a restaurant, I always opted for one. You couldn't mess up a burger. The food was so yummy and delicious. I couldn't help myself. I wanted more, but I wasn't trying to be greedy. Plus, I wasn't the one paying for the meal. As usual, Jeremy paid for our dinner.

"One day I'll pay," I said, which made him chuckle. I would love to reciprocate occasionally. We walked back to the car. "Thank you for a wonderful night."

"Anything for you, my love."

In the car, he started playing music. The nostalgia hit me because my father used to play R&B music all the time growing up. Jeremy started singing out loud and I followed along. He was playing all the throwback songs and I loved it.

As the music filled our souls, my favorite song came on. We shared the same taste in music. I really felt every word of the lyrics to the song. It got me thinking how did I get so blessed. I felt like I had lucky girl syndrome. I mean, look at Jeremy and I! Who would've thought we'd be here together as boyfriend and girlfriend. I was blindsided by it all.

We arrived at our dorm. "I had a wonderful night with you, Afua."

"Me too, you always plan things with intention." As we walked, he gave me a big hug and a kiss. All I could say was, it felt great being around him.

"Good night, my love."

"Good night, sweet dreams."

I walked back to my dorm, and I took off my makeup. I headed to the bathroom to wash my face. After that I put on my pajamas and got ready for bed. I usually didn't sleep right away, so I just watched Instagram reels until I knocked out.

I woke up to a missed phone call from my mom. It was around 10:30 in the morning and I was still tired.

I FaceTimed her and she picked up on the first ring.

"How come you didn't respond when I called you?"

"Mommy, don't be like that now, I was sleeping."

"Aye Afua woda dodo. You sleep too much."

"It's the weekend. I like to use these days as a chance to relax from my schedule."

"I called to check up on you and ask how things are going in school."

"Everything is fine, no need to worry about me."

"So, do you have a boyfriend, or are dating around?"

"I have a boyfriend."

"Hallelujah, the Lord has done it!"

"Mom, you're overreacting, but I know it's a big deal to you."

"I was hoping you would date in college, but always remember to be careful. I can't wait to meet him."

I was thinking, *Chill out lady, we've only been dating for four weeks.* "Mommy, I still need to know him some more."

"Anyways, your siblings miss you." I have been so caught up in my own life that I forgot about them. "Chloe asks for you every day."

I practically raised her when I was growing up. She was twelve. I got so emotional because I hadn't been away from my family this long. I loved my family so much; without them I wouldn't be here. "Tell Chloe I can't wait to see her for Thanksgiving break."

"I will, and I need to pray for you as well, Afua. May God bless you in everything you do. May he make you strong and protect you against any plan of the enemy. In Jesus' name I pray, amen. Bye, I love you."

"I love you too, Mommy."

I decided that I would get dressed and head to The Circle. I got there and it was closed, so I headed to Griddles and got myself chocolate chip pancakes, eggs, and bacon. The wait wasn't that long because barely anyone was up currently except to go to the library. I headed back to my room, and I saw that Melissa was up. She gave me a look yet again.

I began to think something was wrong with her.

Then she said, "You know your man was in my Instagram inbox hitting on me? I think you should know that before wasting your time."

I was like, *Hmm, she must be lying.* I texted Jeremy and asked to speak to him in person.

He asked what happened and I said, "Can you stop by my dorm? I need to ask you something."

In a blink of an eye, he was at my dorm. "Melissa is accusing you of trying to get with her."

"It is not true. If you don't believe me, check my phone. She was telling me how she's interested in me. I don't even know how she found my Instagram." He showed me and in fact Melissa had been texting him. He told her he had a girlfriend and that's when she threatened to tell me.

I had never been so mad in my life. I spun around to where Melissa still sat and walked up to her. "Stop! Trying to ruin my relationship! Find something better to do with your life!"

That's when we got into a screaming match. Jeremy tried to stop us, but it didn't work. I could feel him trying to pull me away from going next to her. Before I knew it my RA was at the door.

"Hey ladies, I got a noise complaint about commotion coming from your room. We need to have a meeting immediately."

"Bye, Jeremy."

"Bye. Be careful, Afua, remember what I told you."

Melissa and I walked into Stacy's room and it was so beautiful. She had it decked out in gray and white. It smelled nice too; an aroma of sweets filled the air. Almost made me forget why I was there. Melissa and I both sat down in front of one another.

"I wanted to know what's going on with you both."

"With all due respect Stacy, Melissa is trying to ruin my life. She's always having an attitude with me and now she's trying to interfere with my relationship."

"Okay, I see. Melissa, is there anything you want to add to that?"

"Life is stressful for me, and this is stemming from my parents getting a divorce this year and that I just broke up with my boyfriend." Then she began crying. I didn't feel one bit sorry for her. She was playing the 'woe is me' character and I was not having it.

"I'm sorry that you both aren't happy right now, but you should remember the roommate contract." We filled it out knowing that we must come to a resolution. If we couldn't come to an agreement, then one of us could move out and find another roommate. I wasn't willing to move out now. I just got used to my dorm and it was unfair that I was given this ultimatum. Well, she didn't only say it to me, Stacy said it to both of us. I remembered what Jeremy said and it started to make sense at this moment. Melissa wanted me to move out so she could have her own room. She wanted me to act a fool so people viewed me negatively. I wouldn't give her the chance. I would let it go and be the bigger person. Whatever she was trying to do, it would not work. "You both should try to communicate your issues with one another in a calm manner."

"Stacy, I tried that, but each time I try to communicate with Melissa, she gives me an attitude. How can I live like this?"

"I suggest that both of you talk it out when you're ready and make amends. You don't have to be the best of friends, but you have to coexist."

Melissa didn't say anything, just nodded her head the entire time.

After a while, I just felt as though Melissa and I would never be friends.

"You can leave but keep in mind what I said."

The whole time I was annoyed that Melissa got me out of character.

I decided to go to the lounge to calm down. I took my laptop and phone. I figured I'd call Veronica because she was the only one that understood me the most when I was upset. Once I was in the lounge, I FaceTimed my bestie.

She picked up the phone.

"Sis, you won't believe what just happened."

She was all confused until she uttered, "Does it have to do with your roommate?"

"Bingo, you hit the hammer on the nail."

"What did she do?"

"Melissa tried to break me and Jeremy up."

"Wait, is there something you're not telling me? I'm confused."

"Sorry for skipping details. I should have told you this first, but last night Jeremy asked me to be his girlfriend."

"Wow, that's so awesome! I'm happy for you. Tell me exactly what Melissa did to you."

"Melissa messaged Jeremy and then tried to lie and tell me that he was hitting on her."

Veronica was lost for words.

"What kind of person would do such an evil thing? Sis, I think you need to move out or try to ignore her."

"Veronica, you're right. I should move out, but I really don't want to. Then I guess I'll go with option two, which is to ignore her."

"Melissa is looking for trouble, but doesn't know that you will rise above it. She thinks that her antics will get her somewhere because she's used to getting her way, but this is college—no one cares."

I agreed with Veronica that no one cared about you more than yourself. If she wanted to act like a kid that was her business.

"So, Sis, spill the details on the date you just had."

"Okay girl, I will, hold on. Jeremy and I went to a paint and sip. It was fun painting with him even though he's way better at it then me. He learned my language just to tell me I love you. That's when my heart melted."

"He must be an outstanding guy from what I hear. I pray he keeps giving you reasons to smile."

"Thanks, and yes, he is, and he keeps it real with me because he hates liars. He always looks out for me and gives me advice. Jeremy makes time for me with his busy schedule."

"Those are qualities that he's supposed to have. A man makes time for what he wants and if it's with you, you'll know." Don't accept the bare minimum, was what she was trying to say.

"Veronica, how's school going?"

"Girl, the pressure is getting worse. These classes ain't no joke."

"Tell me about it. I have to study so much, and I still feel behind."

"Me too, Afua. Apart from that, my family is doing well."

"Good to hear, my mom just spoke to me about my siblings missing me. Kind of feel bad for leaving."

"I know it's not easy, but girl, you were one of the blessed ones to go away for school. You'll see your family again."

"You're right about that."

"Afua, I just realized I have to run an errand for my parents. I gotta go, but have a good day and please ignore your roommate. Talk to you later."

"It's okay, talk to you later."

I sat in the lounge and decided to stay here a while longer. When I was upset, I liked to type my feelings in the notes section of my phone. As I typed, I poured out my emotions. After I was done, I felt so good. I realized that I hadn't eaten the food I bought. That's when I decided I'd heat up my food in the basement lounge. I heated up my food and saw that the basement was a nice place to relax. But I just went back upstairs. Once I was back in my room I noticed Melissa was not around. I decided to watch *A Different World* because that show could put me in the best mood.

I binge watched the show for hours until Melissa came into the room. "Hey Afua, can we talk about what happened earlier?"

I really didn't want to hear what she had to say because it'd be a bunch of excuses.

"Whatever you have to say means nothing to me right now."

She started to cry. "That was a tough blow, you hurt my feelings."

If anything, she hurt my feelings when she tried to hit on Jeremy behind my back. I just let her continue playing the victim because I didn't care. I was the victim in all this but you didn't see me crying. In fact, I didn't make excuses like she did. What made her think I wanted to hear her nonsense at this moment?

"We can speak when you stop playing the victim."

"I am sorry." It was a little too late for all that.

I ignored her and went back to watching my show until it was time for me to sleep. I knew I was being mean to her, but you would too if you were in my shoes.

I woke up to my alarm and saw that it's time for me to get ready for class. It was my favorite class so far, psychology. I hurried up and got ready for the day. As I walked to my class, I listened to some '90s jams. I reached class and sat in my seat. I usually sat in the front row because I concentrated better there. Professor Brown hadn't arrived yet. I talked to my classmate, Rochelle.

"Hey girl, do you know what we will be learning today?"

"Let me check my folder for the syllabus, Afua. According to the syllabus, we will be talking about memory."

"Did you read for class?"

"Nope. Did you?"

"That's a no for me too."

That's when we both started laughing. The professor came to class and got settled. He set up the projector and pulled up his PowerPoint. We learned about the three-stage model of memory. We input memory through our senses into sensory memory, then to short term memory, and finally to our long-term memory. When we need to recall our memory, it flowed back to short term memory. It was an interesting class. Professor Brown told the class that we would have an exam about the things we learned thus far.

Rochelle and I walked out of class together and decided we would study together for the exam. Rochelle and I parted ways because she had another class after this. I headed to The Circle to get some food. I decided to eat a cheeseburger with fries and a Brisk iced tea. I paid for my things and headed straight to my room. Once I reached the dorm, I saw Stacy.

"Hey Afua, how are things going from yesterday?"

"Melissa tried to talk to me, but she was playing the victim, so I ignored her."

"I'm not trying to impose my feelings onto you, but I think you should try to hear her out, and if you think it's not genuine then just ignore her. Fighting will not solve anything. It only brings unnecessary tension."

"Thank you for the advice, I'm heading to my room." I changed into my comfy clothes and began watching YouTube. I watched clothing hauls. It made me want to shop for some clothes. In my defense, I went places with Teddy, and I needed nice clothes for those dates. I guessed that was a good enough excuse for me. I got on Shein and began to order some clothes that I put in my shopping cart. I felt so excited, and it didn't cost me that much money either.

After that, I watched more YouTube until I realized that I should start studying. I grabbed my textbook and headed to my desk. I began taking notes on the first few chapters. I was making a study guide based on the book and the PowerPoint slides. The information was interesting, but over time I grew tired. I always got tired doing work in my room, for some odd reason. So, I decided to finish the study guide and work on practicing sign language. That class was my second favorite because it was fun and exciting. I learned that all the male signs were near the forehead. Whereas the female signs were near the chin. I thought that was very interesting. I also wondered why the rules were like that. I started practicing how to sign my first and last name. I got pretty good at it too. Eventually I fell asleep. It was a very boring and uneventful day.

The next morning, I walked to work listening to music to give me energy for the day ahead. This was my motivation to go to work. I was in the best mood ever and no one was going to stop it. I arrived at the library, and I saw my good friend McKenzie. We talked for a little bit and then I went straight to my desk. Time passed and I grew bored. Then suddenly, I saw someone approach my desk. Guess who it was? If you guessed Melissa, you guessed right. She needed my help with looking for articles for an assignment.

"Hey, I'm working on an African American studies paper. It's about the impact of racism in the United States."

"Sure, I'll help you, just give me a second to look up some books and articles we have in stock." I didn't want to help her, but I was at work, and I needed to remain professional. It was awkward the whole time. I put aside my feelings and helped her. It wasn't in my heart to be spiteful.

She left and I continued to help more students until my shift was over. I realized that today was the Curly Hair Club meeting. I almost forgot until I saw a flyer for their event on the wall. I was going to this event because they were making DIY hair masks. I went to The Circle and got some food. I chose to get some lasagna, then headed to my dorm. I ate my food while watching African movies. The movie was a romance about friends who turned into lovers. I thought it was an alright movie, but I felt like the main character should've known her ex-boyfriend was no good for her. It took her the majority of the movie to figure that out. It was time for me to go to the club meeting. I walked to the college center and into the room where the meeting was held. I saw that it was filled with people. I saw Stacy and Alyssa, who both said hi to me. I decided to sit near Alyssa. Stacy greeted everyone and introduced herself. She said that they would be teaching us how to make our own hair mask.

The hair mask was made from avocado, extra virgin olive oil, and honey. It was cool making it. Although it got messy. Regardless of that, it was great being able to be around like-minded individuals. We gave each other hair tips and discussed what products worked best for each hair type. I enjoyed myself. Stacy then gave an announcement about their annual hair show that would be happening in November. We were approaching the first week of October so it was happening soon. She mentioned that they needed hair models. I was nervous about agreeing to do it.

Alyssa looked in my direction and said, "Afua, why don't you model for the hair show. It will be fun, and I'll be in it so you will not be alone."

I thought about it for a minute. "I guess It wouldn't hurt to be in the show."

"Great, I'm happy we get to see each other more."

"Me too."

Stacy and her board members were very excited. It was me and a few other girls who wrote our name down to participate in the show. I was filled with nervousness. *What if I fall when I'm modeling?* There I went, overthinking the worst again. I must think positively, because I might enjoy myself.

I left the meeting and headed to my dorm. I randomly began thinking about what my mom said concerning my youngest sister. I FaceTimed Chloe on her iPad and she picked up. She was all happy that I called her.

"Afua, I miss you so much."

"I know, I miss you and everybody so much."

My two other siblings came on the FaceTime call, and they all said, "When are you coming home?"

I didn't mention this before, but I had a brother named Kwabena and another sister named Penelope.

"I'm coming home during Thanksgiving."

"That's a long time from now."

"Chloe, I know, but I'll be home in no time."

"No fair."

"I know, I know." I hadn't talked to them since the day I left for college. I know, I was a bad sister. In my defense, a lot happened to me this past month.

"How's school going?"

"It is getting hectic."

"Wow that's tough, but I know you can do this. I've seen you accomplish so much already."

"I am loving it at school. You won't believe that I'm making friends in 6th grade."

"That's nice you are adjusting well to middle school. Look at you, being a mini celeb at your school." Chloe was in 6th grade while the other two were in 10th and 11th grade. I laughed with Chloe and continued to talk to her until I reached my dorm.

"Okay Chloe, I will talk to you later. Please be a good girl for me, alright?"

"I will, Afua, and promise not to miss us too much up there. Talk to you later."

The moment I opened the door, Melissa saw me and tried to start a conversation yet again. This time I was all ears. I remembered what Stacy told me earlier and applied it to this situation. Melissa said how sorry she was and that she was feeling lonely. *I mean, if you're lonely, get on a dating app. Why would you go after someone who's already taken and threaten them?* I thought.

"I don't understand why you had to go after Jeremy."

"I was jealous of you because my life is terrible right now. I thought you had it all and I wanted you to feel my pain."

"What? Jealous of me, why? I don't have the most perfect life. It might seem that way but sometimes I struggle. The difference between you and me is I'm not malicious to other people when things don't go my way."

"I'm very sorry about what I did to you. I know I betrayed your trust."

"I accept your apology. If God can forgive so can I, but if you ever try that again, we will never speak."

Melissa's eyes grew wide and she was left speechless by what I said, but I was serious. What she was doing was getting out of hand. If she ever tried that again I'd ignore her for the rest of the year. I knew who my real family and friends were. I wasn't at school to endure nonsense from people. If I didn't like something I removed myself from the situation. After our conversation, I watched more African movies until I fell asleep.

I woke up and it was 11 in the morning. I got some good sleep for once, but I wished I would've woken up earlier. I could have started studying for my psychology exam next week. I texted Rochelle and asked her when we would study. We agreed to meet up tomorrow at my lounge. If it got too loud, we could go to the library. I finished getting ready for the day and decided to get a head start on studying. So, I grabbed my index cards and wrote down important vocabulary words. The whole day felt like a blur. I didn't do much other than study and watch *The Chi*.

Self-Awareness

I RANDOMLY HAD THE THOUGHT TO SEE A THERAPIST. LATELY I HADN'T BEEN feeling my best. I felt like I didn't even know who I was. Despite all the good things happening for me, I didn't feel very happy. That's a red flag for me because generally I was a happy person but every now and then I felt bouts of depression. I figured it would be best for me to go to the mental health center. I was greeted by a woman, and she asked how she could help me. I said I would like to schedule a session with a therapist. She asked for my name, ID, and some personal information. Before I knew it, I had an appointment scheduled for the following week. She said that it would be with Dr. Stevens. She told me a few things about therapy and after that I was out the door. I was proud of myself for getting the help that I needed. So many times, African American people and other minority groups felt like mental health shouldn't be talked about. We didn't get the help that we needed and suffered in silence.

I knew that if I wanted to be good mentally, I needed to see a professional. As I walked to The Circle, I had a good feeling about my decision. I remembered that Rochelle and I were supposed to meet up to study. I checked my phone, and I got a message from her asking where I was. I apologized and told her I was on my way. Usually, I was on top of stuff like this. We were supposed to meet in the main lounge of my dorm, but we had a change of plans. I arrived at the library and said hi to my coworkers.

I found Rochelle and she looked at me like, "Girl, where have you been?" Once more I apologized, and we began studying. I showed Rochelle my study guide and she loved how it was color coded for each chapter. She went to the scanner to copy my notes for herself.

We spent the entire two hours studying. During that time, we tested each other on the material. I thought we understood the concepts very well. We decided we would call it quits and study individually before the exam. I found out that she lived in the Bronx, but her parents immigrated from Barbados. She was also a psychology major. So, it looked like we would be having classes together.

Two days passed and I realized that while I tried to take care of my mental health, I should also focus on my physical health. I planned on getting a gym membership. Afterwork, I headed to the gym. I was greeted by one of the staff, named Marley, and signed up for a gym membership.

"Can I be paired with a personal trainer?"

"Do you have a preference on whether your trainer is male or female?"

"I would prefer female."

"What are your goals?"

"I would like to tone my physique."

"Well, I have set you up with a trainer who will meet with you when you choose to come back to the gym. Have a wonderful day."

"You too." I left the gym feeling accomplished. I did something I never thought I would in college. I was usually the type that avoided the gym because of my self-consciousness. Whenever I used to work out, it would be at home because I could control the environment. I've heard of the freshman fifteen, which was where you gained weight due to the food that you're eating the first year of college and possibly after. I wasn't trying to let myself go. So, I would try to stop myself before I lost control. Suddenly, Jeremy texted.

JEREMY:

How's your day going?

ME:

I got a gym membership.

JEREMY:

I'm happy for you taking steps to better yourself. I know you have been worried about your health and physique.

ME:

Yes, I have which is why I needed to do something fast.

JEREMY:

We will go on a date this weekend.

ME:

Where are we going?

JEREMY:

Someplace fun. I will leave you to enjoy the rest of your day. Bye Babe

ME:

Bye have a wonderful day

Something fun? That could mean a million things, but either way, I was excited. This man never ceased to amaze me. The last date we had was fun. So, I could only imagine what was next. I enjoyed going on dates and having someone that truly cared about me on my side. I never thought I'd be in a relationship so soon. I knew it might be late for some people, but to me, everything was happening so fast. I prayed that I was making the right decision. I needed to learn how to just have fun and enjoy my life.

This week had been good, getting to know my classmate Rochelle much better. Besides class I practically never saw her. I thought this was an opportunity for me to make more friends while I was at school. When I was in high school, I used to trust people so much until I got betrayed by someone named Britney. She made rumors about me in tenth grade that were terrible. Britney claimed I stole her boyfriend, which wasn't true. I lost some friends because of her lies. When I confronted her, she pretended like I was crazy. She said she had no idea what I was talking about. Can you believe she tried to befriend me? It's been years since we last spoke and I had no interest in talking to her. That's when I realized that not everyone was a friend. Sometimes people tried to get next to you so they could use you. Then when they're done, they threw you away like trash. It's because of that and subsequent issues that I kept my circle small, but I was learning to let people in.

The following day was great, I woke up in a wonderful mood. I went to work as usual, and the most amazing thing happened. Blake came by and thanked me again for helping her with her assignment. She said without my help, she wouldn't have passed her research topic. She wanted to speak to my boss to give me a promotion, but my boss wasn't around. Plus, I didn't think that's how things worked. I wished I could be promoted for my hard work cause I loved this job. It's the first job that I felt at ease doing. I was really touched by that encounter. It showed that I was doing my job of helping people, which I loved. She also invited me to come to a party off-campus, but I politely declined because I had plans with Teddy. Plus, I didn't do well at parties. I was socially awkward so I normally felt tense in situations outside my norm. Maybe one day in the future, I'd go.

After that, I went to my dorm because I was full from the quick breakfast I had before I came to work. I walked to my room. I relaxed for a few hours until I realized that today was the African student organizations meeting. I ran quickly as I could to the campus center and into the meeting room. It had tons of people in there. I spotted Gabriel and he waved my direction. He told me to sit next to him. During the meeting they were talking about dating and how it's difficult being African. I agreed with some of what was being said.

One girl with a long middle-part hairstyle and beautiful dark skin said, "African parents always want you to focus on school and church. Somehow when you reach twenty-five, suddenly, they want you to start thinking of marriage. They don't want you to have relationships because to them it's a distraction."

I heard the crowd of people saying, "Mm-hmm, that's very true." It's so true; my mom and dad both used to say that having a boyfriend would only divert me from my path in life.

People in the meeting were saying things that I didn't agree with as well.

One of the guys said, "Sex is the most important part of a relationship. If I can't do that, I feel unliked by my partner." I felt like people really agreed with him while others just said no.

A girl wearing a short bob and pink track suit gave a rebuttal to his claim. "I understand your feelings towards intimacy with your partner, but sex is only one part of it. You do not have to have sex to feel loved. Simply spending time with them is enough."

"I would have to disagree with you on this, my sister. Sex is important to me, and you can't change that. It's not enough to just spend time with one another."

Gabriel and I both looked at each other confused at what was going on. A heated debate was going to ensue when they changed the topic. In my opinion I felt like people thought sex was a big thing, but to have true intimacy there needs to be a connection between both parties. That's why I was glad that Teddy didn't pressure me. He understood and agreed that we were both waiting until marriage. It wasn't ideal for most college students, but for me it was. Sex was only a part of intimacy, but there were many types, such as emotional, mental, and spiritual. Jeremy was definitely a keeper, and I hoped we could stay together.

The board of ASO started to ask for people to participate in their fashion show.

Gabriel looked at me and said, "Why don't you model?"

I told him I was already modeling for the hair show. That's when he suggested I do both, but I had to let him know that was too much. After the meeting, the board announced that they would be having Jeopardy the following week. I was excited for the shows coming up this school year. Walking into my dorm, I was thinking about the shows and how fun they would be. As I opened my door, I overhear Melissa yelling at someone on the phone.

"Stay away from me! I don't want you anymore! Don't give me none of your stupid excuses, we are done, remember?"

I figured she was talking to Todd. "Hey, is everything alright with you Melissa?"

"Things aren't going well. Todd keeps calling me from an unknown number trying to explain himself. He said that he loved me and wanted to get back together. Todd even apologized for what he did, but I'm over him. I am currently talking to a guy named Noah. We met at a house party. I told Todd that if he tried to call again, I would file a restraining order against him. That might scare him off."

"Just be careful Melissa, this guy has shown you he doesn't respect your boundaries."

"I will, but he knows not to mess with my family."

I wanted to tell her the first time I met Todd that I knew he ain't the one. I was glad she opened her eyes once he showed his true colors. I was happy she found someone else and moved on from the situation. My only worry was that she might be moving on too fast. Then I realized that everyone coped with things differently and there's no set way to heal. The rest of the night was spent anticipating where I was going the next day with Jeremy. I went to sleep eventually but it was the hardest thing ever. I woke up to a call from none other than my mom. It was 9 am.

"I called to ask if everything is alright."

"I have exciting news. I'll be going on a surprise with Jeremy."

She lit up with excitement; I could tell by the intonation in her voice. "He's a good guy, taking you to different places. I wonder where he's taking you?" I was very pleased that she liked him. Now I must get my dad to like him too, once I told him.

"Yes, he is. Mommy, the suspense is bothering me."

"Have fun. I pray you have a wonderful day and that everything goes well for you. In Jesus' name I pray, amen."

"Talk to you later, Mommy."

My mom loved to pray for me any chance she got. It's one of her love languages which was words of affirmation. I appreciated it because it showed she cared about my wellbeing.

In a hurry, I ran to the bathroom to quickly shower and get ready. I finished everything in under an hour which was fast for me. I settled on wearing a pink shirt with jean shorts paired with my favorite pink crocs with jibbitz on them. I told Jeremy that I was ready and he told me to wait for him by the front desk. I went and a few minutes later, he came out dressed in jeans and a white shirt with a gold chain. He wore Nike Air Max shoes. When Jeremy saw me, he gave me the biggest hug and as usual he smelled so good. He was very happy to see me. As we walked to his car, he kissed me. I felt so safe and loved in his presence.

"Where are we going, buddy?"

He said in a happy tone, "We're going to the aquarium."

I was so filled with joy because I had never been to an aquarium before.

"Are you excited?"

"Heck yeah!"

He started laughing so hard. "Your reaction is pure gold, Afua."

"Why did you choose to take me here?"

"Well, I thought you'd find it interesting and who doesn't like seeing sea animals."

"You have a point there."

As we drove, he played good music from Afrobeats to Caribbean. We were jamming and enjoying ourselves. It was about an eighteen-minute drive. Once we arrived, I was so giddy with excitement. When we went inside to pay for the tickets, we were greeted by a man named Tim. The tickets were $18 per adult. Plus, if you wanted to feed the stingrays, it was an additional $10. There was also a reptile show that would happen later. I wanted to get the whole experience. During our time there we saw different types of fish. There was a red lion, white koi, and puffer. I even saw fish that reminded me of Nemo and Dory. This included fishes from Thailand, Tokyo, and west coast California. They had eels, turtles, lobsters, crabs, sea urchin and jellyfish. There were sharks as well but the coolest of the bunch were the leopard shark. We had the opportunity to see stingray fish and touch them.

At first, I was very scared, but after a while my nerves went away. We also went through a tunnel that was amazingly beautiful. It has different kinds of fishes and sharks swimming all over. Jeremy suggested we take a picture together. We asked someone passing by to take our picture, which came out adorable. I asked Jeremy if he wanted to go to the reptile show and he said yes. During the show we saw a bearded dragon, tarantula, and ball python. There were other reptiles, but I didn't know the names of them. I got to see them up-close, which was cool. After that, we entered the gift shop and got some knick-knacks. It was a great time being with my favorite person. He really knew how to make me forget about my problems. We then decided that we'd go to an Asian restaurant called Azuma Sushi Bistro. We both got hibachi and had the chef cook in front of us which was great. I got a Fanta drink while babe got a Coke. In addition to this we both ordered miso soup. I realized how much I loved seeing people cook in front of me. The cook was very entertaining. He kept cracking jokes.

Once we finished eating, we went in the car to drive back to Albany.

"It was a great time! I love you so much, Jeremy."

He was in shock. "For real, you love me?"

"Yes, I do!" I exclaimed. I thought this made our relationship stronger despite only being together for a week.

We began jamming to old '90s music. My favorite song came on, "Waterfalls" by TLC, and I began singing from the top of my lungs. I liked the part when Left Eye raps. Her words encouraged me. I really felt that in my soul. We arrived on campus ten minutes later.

"I love you so much, Afua, you're a queen in my eyes."

"Aww, thank you, and I see you as my king love." He made me feel so happy, to know that he saw me that way meant everything to me.

"I'm not perfect, but I'm glad that you see the best in me. I will always stay by your side. It doesn't matter where life takes us, you will always have a piece of my heart." I didn't know he could be so romantic and loving with his words.

The day wasn't over, and I still wanted to spend time with him. So, I suggested we watch a movie or TV show in the lounge. He agreed. We walked to the dorm and into the main lounge. There was no one in the lounge. Jeremy said he would bring his laptop and hook it up to the television. When he came back from his room, he set up the laptop. Then put on Netflix. We agreed upon a '90s movie classic called *Clueless*. You know, the one where the main character Cher falls for her ex-stepbrother Josh. I always thought that part was weird despite it being a popular movie, but I remembered there being a show as well. We watched the movie and enjoyed Cher play matchmaker with two of her teachers. After the movie was over, we talked.

"How have you been feeling lately, Jeremy?"

"I have been feeling stressed."

"I understand you on that. However, I have been feeling home-sick and sad."

"Keep calm, this feeling will pass. We all get homesick, but it doesn't last for long."

"How's exam studying going for you?"

"It seems hard, but I'm getting the hang of the concepts. I even created a study guide and had a study partner."

"You're doing all the right things. You will pass, just believe in yourself."

I was working hard. There's an African proverb that said, "Knowledge is like a garden if not cultivated, it cannot be harvested." Education was important to me, which was why I worked hard. You must constantly educate yourself in life to reap the true fruits of life. Before I knew it, it was two hours later and we had talked about everything under the sun. We decided to go and relax in our rooms. He walked me to my room and gave me a hug and kissed my forehead. At that moment I felt sad because I enjoyed spending every moment with him. I knew I'd miss being around him this week. I was being a little over dramatic but that's how I felt right now. For the rest of the day, I just watched *The Chi*. I missed so many episodes that I needed to catch up on.

The next two days were spent going to work and studying for my Psychology exam. It was pretty uneventful. I studied so much that I got a headache. Anyways, the following day I went to therapy, and it was nerve-wracking at first. I was greeted by a woman named Olivia. She told me to fill out some forms. Then when I was done, I got on the computer and filled out an assessment to see if I had suicidal tendencies. According to Olivia, it was a prevention method in case I might be of harm to myself. They didn't play when it came to mental health. I knew I wasn't a danger to myself. I anticipated my turn in the waiting area for approximately twenty-five minutes. I was greeted by a woman who introduced herself as Dr. Stevens. She was of African American descent and average build. She wore nice glasses and had long locs. She was so inviting and friendly, greeting me with a smile. Dr. Stevens told me to sit down in the chair then began to ask me some questions.

"Why did you decide to go to therapy?"

"I was homesick and feeling down about it. I figured that it would be best to find someone to talk to about my situation."

"That is okay, because I'm here to help you. What are you hoping to achieve from therapy?"

"I want to work on my self-defeating thoughts about my life. I want to cope with being away from home and work on my happiness."

"These are good things to work on. I have noticed that not everyone has introspection on their weaknesses. Let's talk about confidentiality. What we talk about stays here unless it involves the harm of yourself, another person, or a minor."

I began to speak. At first, I felt nervous to express myself, but she allowed me to talk about my feelings. "I try to be the best at everything academically, and it's taking a toll on my mental health."

"Where do you think that behavior came from?"

"I guess from a young age, I have been pushed to be the best at everything which is a good thing, but that also puts so much pressure on me. My parents want me to get straight A's and if I don't, they are hard on me. Being the oldest means I am the example for my younger siblings."

"How does that make you feel?"

"I don't know. I guess it makes me feel stressed because I'm seen as an example for others. It makes me frustrated because I often fall short of my parents' expectations."

"I see. The expectations your parents have on you matter the most. When you don't meet them, it makes you feel like a disappointment."

I thought, *Hallelujah, someone understands me on a deeper level.*

"Exactly! That's what I have been trying to say. I feel like I have to be some kind of example all the time, and no one wants to hear when I'm struggling. I hate to talk about my shortcomings 'cause if I do, I'm afraid people will view me as a loser. There's only a select few I share my most intimate fears with, but not often. I should be happy about all the things that I've accomplished but I'm not. I always feels as though I should be doing more."

"What more do you think you should do?"

"I think I should be successful already, as crazy as that seems. I wonder when my life will start being exciting for me."

"You are exactly where you're meant to be in life. If things were supposed to be different, it would have already happened. I want you to be happy for your achievements because you worked hard for them."

"I agree with you. It's always good to reflect on your wins in life."

"Are you in a relationship or dating?"

"I am in a relationship with a guy named Jeremy and he's the best. I'm so grateful for him."

"I'm happy for you. Our time together is up, but we will meet again next week."

I was sad because I wanted to talk to her more. In spite of this, I was also happy that I found a counselor that understood me.

I walked back to my dorm room when I remembered that I got a notification about my package. I went to my mail room and was greeted by a girl named Luisa. She asked me what I needed help with, and I told her about my package. She found it and handed it to me. I was so filled with joy because I'd been waiting for it for a while. I thanked her and headed straight to my room. I began trying on some of my clothes and they all looked good on me. I figured that I would use the clothes for date nights with Teddy because we went to a lot of places together. I realized I spent a lot of money. I needed to slow down on buying clothes for a while. I had a shopping obsession. When I had spare time, I went on Shein and Amazon and browsed their websites. I knew I shouldn't do this but it was so hard not to. When I was living in Brooklyn, I always had packages coming to the house every week. Don't ask how I had all that money to buy things back then because even I don't know.

After I finished trying on clothes, I reviewed my study guide. This took me a couple of hours. The realization came that I was fully prepared for the exam. Although on the other hand, I was feeling a bit nervous that I might fail the exam. I knew I prepared and had studied so hard for it, but I feared my efforts wouldn't be enough. I always did this before an exam, which was self-defeating. It caused me to second-guess my abilities. That was my first college test, and I didn't know what to expect. I remembered in high school, I was given the opportunity to take college courses in advance, but I refused. It was due to the amount of stuff on my plate. Looking back, I should have taken advantage of college courses. It would have given me a feel of the coursework. As I studied, I grew tired rereading the same words over and over again. That's when I knew it was time to call it a night. I then went to sleep so that I could be alert during the test.

Today was the day of my exam and nervousness came over me again. I made sure I woke up early. I started my day with breakfast from the dining hall. Then I walked to class. The whole time I was thinking, *what if I fail?* Then I realized that negative thinking would cause me to perform poorly. I entered the lecture and saw that Professor Brown was there, but the class was missing some students. I sat down one seat apart from Rochelle.

"Do you feel prepared for the exam?"

"Girl, nope."

"Wow, I was feeling the same way."

"Well, good luck."

"Good luck to you too. May the odds be in our favor."

Professor Brown handed out the test and told us we would have the full three hours to complete it. I got my test and immediately started. I told myself I understood the concepts well enough to pass the exam. I answered the questions I knew first and then went to the ones I was unsure about. There was a short answer question that caught me off guard. Before I knew it, I was done with the exam and headed out the door. It took me two hours and thirty minutes to finish. I felt drained after. I went to The Circle to grab a bite to eat before heading to my dorm. To reward myself, I binge watched *True Crime Documentaries* on Netflix.

The next day started off good. I was listening to a podcast which was outside my norm. Usually, I listened to music in the morning. This podcast was a motivational start to my morning. I finished getting ready for the day. An hour passed by, and I got a text from Rochelle.

"Girl, did you look on Blackboard? Professor Brown just posted the exam scores."

"What, he did?!Let me check."

I got on Blackboard, and it showed my grade was a 97. I was so happy I began jumping up and down. I told Rochelle my grade and she told me she got a 95. I was so ecstatic that we both passed with high scores. We both agreed that we would continue to be study buddies. I then called my parents and told them that I passed. They were so filled with joy, but they asked me how come I didn't get a 100. At that moment, I was a bit taken back because I don't know the reason why. I told them that the test was very difficult, and I tried my best.

That's when my parents said, "Next time, you'll get higher than that, in Jesus's name."

After I got off the phone with them, I texted Teddy and told him I passed. He was overjoyed and said that he figured I'd do well 'cause I was intelligent and hardworking.

He told me that tomorrow he had a surprise for me. I was like, *oh my! I wonder what it could be?*

As usual, he said it would be something that he knew I would enjoy. I could only imagine what it would be. He had my imagination running thinking about it. I loved how he cared about me and planned these dates. I wanted to do something special for him one of these days. Maybe when I went to Brooklyn for Thanksgiving or Christmas break, I could finally plan something. I was thinking about taking Teddy to the Museum of Ice Cream. I thought that would be cool. After telling people the news, I decided to get ready for work. I walked to the library and when I arrived, I immediately said hello to everyone. I saw McKenzie and we talked for a little bit. We hadn't seen one another for a while, since we worked on different floors. Today I had to go to the third floor. I used that opportunity to work on my math assignment. I was starting to get the hang of math ever since I decided to get a tutor. The person that was tutoring me always got me to understand the concepts before our session was over.

As I sat, a few people came, asking for help with their assignments, which I gladly assisted. Soon after, there was a rush of people that came all of a sudden. Time flew by fast and before I knew it, my shift was over. I went to The Circle to buy some food. I got chicken stir-fry and headed to my dorm. I thought my schedule was becoming predictable now which was quite sad. I did the same thing all the time except on weekends. I was so excited for tomorrow; I wondered what was in store for me. I headed to my dorm and once inside, I noticed that Melissa was there. She was in a cheerful mood.

She greeted me and then asked, "How's your day?"

"Fine."

"That's nice, Afua. Everything is working out for me. My hockey team has been doing well in their tournaments." She was so happy to tell me the news. "I am having fun dating Noah. He is definitely an upgrade from Todd, and he actually treats me with the respect I deserve. Since that day I told Todd off, he's been trying to call or text me from different numbers trying to get my attention. He said a restraining order will not scare him away, but I'm not scared of him."

I feared for her life because men like him could be dangerous. "I am elated that you are doing well. My only issue is Todd. You should take precautions to protect yourself."

"You don't have to worry about me because he's scared of my dad and won't dare try anything."

"I suggest you still look into a restraining order, since it appears that he's obsessed with you. I am very concerned that he'll do something harmful."

"I'm fine, trust me."

"I hope all will go well, because this man seems unwell."

"If anything happens to me, are you going to stand by me?"

I was a bit hesitant to answer, but I said yes because I didn't like seeing people get hurt around me. My parents taught me to always stand for what was right. I couldn't sit around while someone was getting abused and used. It wasn't in my nature. Plus, we were back on speaking terms. I had already forgiven her and gave her a warning to never try to interfere with my love life. It seemed that she listened. We talked about other things but it all circled back to me telling her to be careful. In my eyes it seemed as though she wasn't taking things seriously. Then I remembered that we were all processing the world and situations through different lenses. I thought because of that she wasn't seeing the situation for what it truly was. For the rest of the day, I read and worked on my sign language. I'd learned to form sentences which I thought was amazing. Sign language was so expressive in nature, and I loved it.

This was the morning of my date with Jeremy. I was still curious but I knew it would be someplace fun. I got a text from him telling me to be ready by 12pm. Since it was 10:30am, I figured I should get ready for the date. I headed to the bathroom and took a shower. I used my favorite products and then I went back to my dorm room. I wished we had a bathroom in each dorm room so we could have our own privacy and not have to clean up after other people. But I guessed this would do for now. I told myself that today I was going to look good. So, I put on some makeup which took me forever to do. I wore a pink bodycon dress with a heart shaped neckline. I was feeling so much myself. I couldn't contain my excitement for today.

Melissa was awake and she told me, "Girl, you look good."

"Thank you, I try."

I smiled from ear to ear. That was the first time she said something nice to me. I guessed I was wrong about her. Perhaps we could be cordial with one another.

It was time for me to meet Jeremy. I walked to the main lounge, and I saw him waiting for me. He was wearing a blue button-down collar shirt with matching pants.

"Babe, you are looking like a queen."

I began smiling again. "Aww, really? You think so? Thank you." Jeremy had a joyful presence about him, and his facial expression warmed my heart.

"Babe, you ready?"

"Of course." We headed out. As we were inside the car, Jeremy told me that we would be going on a picnic. I was hype. You couldn't stop this mood I was in. He drove us to McDonald's. I ordered a spicy chicken sandwich with large fries and Jeremy got a quarter pounder with cheese and bacon and large fries. I saw that he had some bags in the back seat. I was guessing that it was our food for the date. Jeremy drove to Washington Park which was roughly eleven minutes from where we were. When we arrived, I was amazed by the flowers I saw. They were so beautiful. We walked through the park and found a nice spot to lay our blanket down. I saw all the food that Jeremy brought. It turned out that he planned a rainbow themed picnic. We had various snacks from different color groups. For pink snacks we had frosted animal crackers and pink Starburst. Next was yellow, we had golden Oreos, Lays, Funyuns, peanut M&Ms. After that, we had the blue colored snacks which was blue Oreos, Rice Krispie treats, and Welch's fruit snacks. Next was purple, and for that we had Kool-Aid jammers and Takis. Then we had orange, which was Reese's, cheddar Pringles and Cheez-Its. Finally, we had the color green, which was sour cream Lay's chips, sour Skittles, and Go-Go Squeeze.

"Wow, you surpassed my expectations. This is a lot for two people."

After we finished setting up everything, I saw Jeremy pull out a bunch of flowers from out of nowhere. I guessed I didn't notice because I was busy placing the snacks down on the blanket.

"I love you so much. I wanted to show my appreciation to you for being a great girlfriend. You are the best thing that happened to me in a while. I wanted to let you know how special you are to me."

Tears began to fall from my eyes. One thing that my friends and family told me was that I was very sensitive. If I really loved and cared about the person, I'd cry if they told me something heartfelt. We kissed and time stopped for a second. In his arms I felt safe.

"I love you because of how you care for me. I won't ever take advantage of your kind heart. It will hurt me to my core to ever see you sad because of my actions. I have reassurance that you won't take advantage of me that's why I want to give you the world."

We shared a lovely moment together.

"I can't imagine life without you in it."

"Me too. You gave me a new perspective on love, Jeremy." What do I know about love, being that it was my first relationship, but I knew how I felt. If anyone was in my shoes, they would feel the same for their partner.

I admired the flowers, trees, and the sky. As I sat, I felt one with nature. It was a great thing to do with Teddy. I enjoyed every minute of my time.

"My week was so busy. Between classes, work, and clubs, I barely got to relax."

I felt so bad for him 'cause he was so hard-working. "I am so sorry you had a stressful week."

"That's okay, I look forward to the weekend since I get to hang out with you."

We played a game where we asked one another random questions.

He asked me, "What is your favorite snack?"

"Reese's peanut butter cup. You?"

"I would have to say mine is Twix." He happened to buy me my favorite snack and didn't even know it.

"What is your favorite food?"

"Pelau, which is chicken combined with rice, vegetables, fresh herbs, and coconut milk."

"I love to eat jollof rice with goat meat and stew."

"What is your favorite color?"

I loved the color pink. My whole aura radiated pink.

"Ha-ha, I figured you loved that color because your

room is decked out in pink stuff! I love the color green and have some elements of it in my room, but I certainly can't compete with you."

"What's your love language?"

"My love language is physical touch and acts of services. Essentially, the use of body language to express love and doing something your partner would like."

"Mine are words of affirmation and quality time, which involves communicating love and respect for one another and expressing love with undivided attention."

After this, we gathered our things and walked back to the car. It was a great time with him and something I would cherish because he didn't have to do that for me. We spent the rest of the day together, which I enjoyed.

Before the Storm

Days passed and I got in a rut of going to class and work. Ya girl needed a break from it all. Just when I was thinking things couldn't get better, I got a text from Jeremy saying I should get ready tomorrow for a date. Sometimes he surprised me but this time he decided to tell me where we were headed. He told me that we would be going to a farmer's market. Mind you, I had never been to one before. You know, living in the city, you rarely see things like this. Although they're becoming more popular these days. Over there we could pick apples and pumpkins. I spent the rest of the day doing what I loved most, which was laying down and watching African movies on my iPad. It was a great night relaxing since I hadn't done it in a while. The next morning arrived. I was super pumped for the day and had so much energy. I quickly showered and got myself ready. I put on a long-sleeved burnt orange ruched t-shirt and high waisted jogger pants with black Nike sneakers. I waited a few minutes and then walked to the main lobby to meet Jeremy. I saw him and all I could think was, *he's looking fine.* He had a fresh haircut and was wearing a pink shirt with the word *adventure* written in cursive. In addition, he had on khaki cargo pants with black Nike Air Force Ones. We both complimented each other. I made a joke that he was copying my style 'cause he had on Nike sneakers and similar styled pants. He just laughed.

We walked to the parking lot and got in the car. Jeremy was all lovey-dovey with me. He was more romantic with his words. What he did next changed the trajectory of our relationship. He pulled out a necklace and it had one of the adinkra symbols named gye Nyame. In my language Twi, it translated to *except God.* When he did that, I knew right then and there that he loved me. He got me something that came from the heart, and I appreciated it so much. You know I began crying.

He was telling me that he did research and learned about the symbols. He figured I'd like the one about God. He said, and I quote, "It's a reminder that even in your toughest moments, God is there."

In that moment I loved him even more. As he put the necklace on me, I felt so much joy. My heart was full. After that we listened to Afrobeats. We begin singing along to R2bees. It was a vibe the whole car ride to the farmer's market. Once we arrived, I saw that there were so many people. We paid for our tickets and began on our quest. Jeremy told me that they had a cornfield maze we could check out first. We walked over to the field and began our journey through the maze.

We kind of got lost figuring out which way to go. There was a central spot in the maze that had a giant structure where you could climb up and take pictures. We marveled at the vast amount of corn that was around. Eventually we found the structure and took pictures together. It was a fun time trying to figure out how to navigate the field. Now the next thing we had to do was figure our way out. It was very difficult. It felt like we were walking in circles until finally we found the exit. Then we went on a truck ride to the apple tree field. The ride was fairly quick yet bumpy. I kept holding onto Jeremy because I was afraid.

He just started laughing and said, "Babe, it's not that bad."

The apple field had different kinds of red apples such as Honey Crisp, McIntosh, Gala and Red Delicious. Jeremy asked a passerby if they could take our picture. We looked so good in those photos. We picked a few apples, but I was upset that they didn't have Granny Smiths, which were my favorite of all time. We then walked over to the pumpkin patch. I found one that was the right size for my desk. Jeremy had the idea for us to carve and decorate pumpkins for Halloween.

After we were done, we put our stuff in the trunk and headed to the store. I got so enticed by the aroma in the store, it smelled so good. There was a wide array of food and pastries. I got apple cider donuts which made my mouth water looking at it. I wanted to buy the whole store, but Teddy stopped me. He said we shouldn't waste money on stuff we wouldn't eat. I agreed because I tended to buy food for later that I never end up eating. We noticed the store had homemade ice cream. Jeremy asked me if I wanted some. I nearly screamed as I said yes to his question. I picked salted caramel while Jeremy got brown sugar vanilla bean. We thought it would be best for us to eat our ice cream outside before getting into the car. We both enjoyed our ice cream. Although we both would've loved to have gotten toppings, but they didn't have any. We got inside the car and headed to a restaurant. We ended up going to The Cheesecake Factory despite us being underdressed. The waiter we had was so nice and friendly with us. His name was Isaiah. He kept joking around with us. I had the bee sting flatbread pizza. It had Italian sausage, pepperoni, and bacon. There was a spicy kick to it; that's when I realized that it included chiles. Teddy had a cacio e pepe pasta which consisted of spaghetti, Romano, and parmesan. We had a wonderful time talking about our experience at the farmer's market.

Jeremy drove us back on campus. The whole time we listened to some more Afrobeats. We were jamming to songs by King Promise, Omah Lay, and Burna Boy. All I could say is it was a vibe the whole ride back. Jeremy and I bonded over music on a level only we understood. It was the key to my heart. I could listen to songs and instantly my mood changed. Once we arrived on campus, we sat in the car for a little bit just embracing one another's existence. We enjoyed each other's company for a little while longer. Jeremy was telling me that he loved me and wanted us to continue to grow in love with each other. I noticed that he was dedicated to maintaining our relationship. He always considered my feelings. After our moment together, we walked to the dorm carrying our things from the market. I thanked babe for a wonderful time and before you know it, I was off to my room. I was a bit sad because I wanted to spend more time with him. Melissa asked me how my day was. I told her it was amazing and that we went to a farmer's market with a corn maze and apple field. She was happy and said how fun that must've been. She also told me how she was going out soon with Noah. I was beyond ecstatic for her since she moved on from her ex.

I spent my time reminiscing over the day I just had and being excited for the next time I get to see Jeremy. He always shifted my mood and made it better. I thanked God every day that I met an amazing man like him. When I was younger, I used to imagine what my boyfriend would be like. I practically wrote what I wanted in a guy just a few months ago. If you told me I'd meet someone like Jeremy, I'd laugh in your face and call you crazy. I could smell the apple cider scent through the box. I opened the box and took one. It was the best donut I'd ever tasted. When I told you it was moist and delicious, I really meant that. I watched *Mean Girls* to pass the time. I thoroughly enjoyed watching the movie.

Time passed and I got a FaceTime call from Veronica. She was all smiles; when she was like that I knew Veronica had good news.

"Girl, who got you smiling so hard?"

She paused before spilling the tea.

"I met a guy in biology class, Aiden. He sits next to me in the lecture hall. We got to talking...and he just asked me out on a date!"

My mouth dropped! I was so in shock, but in a good way. She finally met a guy that she liked. Well, we both did.

"Earth to Afua. Are you okay? You've gone silent."

"I'm beyond happy for you. I'm delighted. Give me the details on this guy."

"He's tall and lighter in complexion. He is from Mali, West Africa, which is perfect because I always imagined dating a fellow African."

"OMG WOW!" If you know that inside joke, you're a real one. We both started laughing. "Sis, I was waiting for you to go on another date."

"It will be better than my last date."

"I agree, because the other guy was a waste of time. We need to figure out what you're going to wear."

Veronica loved to dress modest. So, we had to find something she'd feel comfortable wearing. She showed me some of her clothing options. We settled on a puff sleeve belted dress that was burnt orange. It was so beautiful and complimented her skin tone. She had on curly deep wave hair which tied the look together. If all went well, we could double date one day. She was hopeful that day would come.

"What are some tips for a successful date? I'm so nervous thinking about it."

"Be yourself and have fun, the date will go well." We talked about wearing makeup and I said, "Do what makes you happy. You are beautiful regardless."

We discussed being homesick. Veronica advised me to remain strong and that I'd be home in no time. I was thankful for the people I had in my life, like Veronica. I came to the realization that it was getting late. We said our goodbyes and I wished her luck on her date with Aiden. Shortly after, I fell asleep. I tried to stay asleep, but it was very difficult. I kept tossing and turning. I woke up a bit groggy the next morning. I decided that I wanted to spend more time with Jeremy. So I called him.

"Babe, what's up? Is everything alright?"

"I was hoping to hang out with you today."

He was happy that I wanted to spend more time with him. He said, "Why don't we grab lunch in the afternoon? We can meet up in the main lobby."

I quickly got ready and waited for him. Moments later, I got a text from him asking if I was ready. I ran to the main lobby. Jeremy smiled when he saw me. When we got outside he paused for a second and looked me in the eyes.

He said, "Babe, are you okay? I can tell something is bothering you."

I was confused because I didn't think he would notice. I guess my demeanor was different. I mean, he's right. Something felt off with me and I couldn't pinpoint what it was. Sometimes I felt like I wasn't myself. I cried for no reason at all and these days I hardly ate. I felt like I was losing myself. That spark was gone, and I wasn't interested in things I normally would be. I felt this before. My depression was coming back. My whole world was crashing. I felt like there was no way out. I didn't want to worry him about that stuff. He already had a lot on his plate.

"I'm just tired, I didn't have enough sleep last night."

He was very worried about me. He kept asking if I was alright. We entered the dining hall and was greeted by one of the staff.

Once we got our food and sat down, I finally decided to come clean and tell Jeremy the truth.

"I haven't been feeling like myself for a while."

"What do you mean?"

I continued, "I've been feeling homesick and it's making me sad. I have struggled with depression in the past, but I haven't been diagnosed."

He told me that I should see a counselor about it. I told him that I had been seeing a therapist and that she had been helping me talk through my feelings. He was happy for me but a bit saddened that I hadn't told him about it.

"I'm sorry—I didn't mean to keep things from you."

"You can always confide in me about anything. We are in a relationship, so your problems are mine. I will be here for you no matter what. Just know you have me." He also said that I should take it easy and do whatever sparked joy. I would try but it wouldn't be easy.

Depression wasn't something that you got over easily; it's something you worked through. We talked and I poured out my feelings to him. I felt heard and understood. That's when he told me that he has a family member who had a mental illness. He saw the challenges they went through to remain mentally stable. He said that I shouldn't be ashamed because it was normal to struggle, and that I shouldn't dwell on it. After that we walked back to the dorm. He gave me a hug and a kiss. Jeremy reassured me that he was going to stick by my side. He knew that it was tough transitioning to college and dealing with all that came with it. I walked to my dorm room and laid in my bed, watching movies on Netflix.

That's when I heard the door open and it was Melissa. She was with a tall guy with freckles and red hair. Melissa walked over to me and introduced me to Noah. He was very nice and friendly. He said hello and was even telling me about himself. I would later find out that he was a computer science major and also a freshman. I thought he was a great fit for her. She appeared happier around him. Melissa went to pick up her bag and they said bye before heading out.

Moments later I got a phone call from my mom. She was so worried about me, being that I hadn't called in a few days.

She said, "Afua, what's going on with you? Adɛn nti na woamfrɛ me?" (Why haven't you called me?)

"I'm sorry, I've just been so busy with school and work."

"There's no excuse. Family comes first." She proceeded to give me a mini lecture about how it was important to call home.

She asked me how I was feeling, and I broke down and said, "I've been sad a lot. I would be happy when I'm with people, but once I get to my dorm, I get so down."

"My daughter, I don't expect you to be happy all the time, but these period of sadness you're experiencing is not normal. Afua, I think you need to pray more and seek God about this."

I wish my mom knew that prayer was only part of it, that counseling was an option. I prayed about it to no avail. My prayers were unheard, and life seemed bleak. Before my thoughts consume me, I wanted to tell my mom that, but I knew it wouldn't impact her. My parents didn't believe that mental illness existed at times. I knew their feelings would change, but it was hard expressing myself with them. The only thing I heard was pray, pray, and pray. She told me that she would keep me in her prayer, but that I had to seek God for myself. We talked some more and then we said bye to each other.

Two days passed by and it was the same old routine. I went to work and class. I got a knock on the door and it was Stacy. She asked if I would like to join the modeling practice tomorrow. I said yes. We exchanged numbers. I laid on my bed until I realized that I had a paper to write for my English class. The paper was a creative writing assignment of my choice. Thinking of what to write was draining, and the more I thought about it, the angrier I became, which led me to put off the assignment for another time. As I sat in my bed, I grew bored. So, I did what I knew best, which was watching Netflix. I ended up watching *The Parkers*. It was a good distractor. Eventually I went to sleep, but still was unable to stay asleep. I didn't know what was going on with me. I couldn't sleep well through the night.

The next morning, I got ready for my counseling session with Dr. Stevens. I entered the mental health center and sat in the waiting room. I was greeted by Dr. Stevens with a huge grin that lit up once she saw me. I entered her room and the session began.

"I haven't been feeling the best emotionally. I get happy when

I'm around people, but being alone sometimes is hard. I miss being around my family."

"I want to assure you that it's normal to be homesick. I come across tons of students who experience this their first semester of college. Do not think for a second you're alone in this feeling."

"I have periods where I'm feeling good and then I get sad. I can't explain why I'm this way. Sometimes I feel hopeless, thinking I'm a failure."

"I can't diagnose you, but it seems as though you're experiencing a period of depression. You have to take it easy on yourself. I noticed that you've been having negative self-talk. I love this quote from Brené Brown which says, 'Talk to yourself like you would to someone you love.'"

I really felt that. We talked about how to have positive self-talk. She worked on some exercises with me. Before I knew it, the session was over. A few hours passed and I remembered that I had modeling practice for the Curly Hair Club. I got up and quickly ran to the meeting room.

They had already started. Alyssa was so happy to see me.

She gave me a hug. "You came just in time!"

There was music playing. All the girls participating lined up and began modeling one after the other. It was my turn to model. The song they put on was by Flo Milli. I was feeling myself so much. I owned that make-believe runway. I did my little model walk and really enjoyed myself.

I could hear Alyssa saying, "You go girl!"

When I was done, I could see the panel was excited. Alyssa modeled and a lot of people cheered for her in the background, including me. It was a fun time modeling.

When it was all said and done, Stacy came up to me. "I'm so glad you came! You're an amazing model. I know it's out of your comfort zone, but that's a good thing! It'll force you to be more confident in yourself and your abilities."

Walking to my dorm, I felt on top of the world. Modeling cheered me up. It wasn't a cure to how I was feeling, but it sure helped a bit.

The following morning, I had work. As I was walking to the library, I listened to some Afrobeats. The songs I'd been listening to on repeat were African gospel. They were beautifully written songs. Anytime I was down and I thought of these songs, my mood shifted. When I walked in, I greeted the people already there. I saw McKenzie and we talked for a brief second before I headed to my section of the desk. Blake walked by. We talked for a little bit. She invited me to a party tonight and said I could invite some friends. I told her sure because I'd rather do something than spend another night in my dorm. She gave me her number and said to text her when I was ready to go. It was going to be a girl's night out. I walked over to McKenzie and asked her if she wanted to go to a party tonight. Of course, she said yes.

The workday went by pretty fast. I was out the door as soon as my shift was over. I texted Rochelle about the party as well and she also said yes. I grabbed a slice of pizza at The Circle. I entered my dorm and ate while watching Netflix. I made a group chat with the girls in it. I told them that we should meet in front of the campus center. We all agreed to meet at 10 pm. I spent the rest of the time thinking about what to wear. I tried on what seemed like a dozen clothes and I didn't like any of them. Finally, I pulled out this cute floral split hem dress and I loved it. While all this was happening, I realized that I hadn't told Teddy I was going out tonight. I texted him and said I was going to a party with some friends. He told me to be safe and that he had a date planned for us the following day at noon. I immediately became excited.

Fast-forward a few hours and it was time to get ready. I put on my makeup and all I could say was I looked good. I wore my dress and walked to the campus center. I see Rochelle waiting in front. She was so happy to see me. Shortly after, Blake and McKenzie walked over. I introduced them to one another, and we walked to the house party.

The apartments weren't too far from the campus. As we got to the party, I heard music blasting. We entered the house and there was a bunch of people there. The people who I assumed were hosting the party were asking us if we wanted to drink. I said no, because for one I was underage and two, I didn't really like the taste of alcohol. Blake and McKenzie decided to drink while Rochelle said no. The guys gave them each what appeared to be jungle juice. I was going to enjoy myself regardless of if there was liquor in my system. We were vibing to the music and dancing. A guy came up to me wanting to dance but I declined the offer. So, he went on to dance with Blake. I didn't feel any particular way about it since I already had a boyfriend. I really enjoyed myself. Rochelle and I talked the whole night and danced with one another. Guys kept coming to us wanting to dance, which I found to be annoying. McKenzie was in her own world, dancing with some guy.

We stayed there until 1 am. I could tell that McKenzie and Blake were a little buzzed. Rochelle and I made sure they returned to their dorm rooms safely. I considered myself to be a loyal friend to the ones I cared about. I was the type of friend that would make sure you were alright since anything can happen at night. I cared about people so much that I couldn't let something happen to them. I knew if I was in that situation, I would want someone to help me too.

Rochelle and I gist about the night and how it was a stress relief from school. We never had nights like this. She said she hoped we could hang out more and I agreed. I walked her to her dorm and then walked to mine. It was a short distance, so I didn't mind. I was more than excited for the day I would have in a few hours. I tried to fall asleep but couldn't. I stared up at the ceiling waiting for tiredness to enter my system. I needed to find a resolution to my problem. I woke up so many times, to the point I thought I was going crazy. I was waiting in anticipation for the day ahead of me. I was very ecstatic thinking about it at one point. However, it was the third time I woke up that I began feeling cranky. Then I thought to myself, *what if I ruin my date with Jeremy because I'm not feeling my best? What if I snap on him and disrupt the mood?* I already opened up to him about my issues, I didn't want to worry him even further. Should I keep this to myself? I needed to talk to my therapist about this again because this wasn't normal.

The next morning Jeremy texted me, asking if I was ready for our date. I told him to give me a few minutes. It was only 11 am. I took a shower and tried to find some clothes to wear. He hadn't told me where we were going yet so I opted for something casual. I wore a color blocked beige ribbed long-sleeved crop top with a black cut out waisted flare leg knit pants. I also had on white and black Adidas. I waited for Jeremy in the main lobby and when he came down the hallway, he was smiling at me. He wore a black and beige flannel with a black tee, his gold chain, and some black jeans. He's also wearing white Air Forces. He gave me a hug and a kiss. It sent me over the moon. I joked with him about copying my style.

"Jeremy, who told you to match with me again?" I guess we've become that kind of couple that matches accidently.

He starts laughing and saying, "Babe, I think you're copying me."

"Whatever, we all know who's copying who today."

We walked over to the car, and I said, "Are you going to tell me what today's adventure is?"

"Are you ready for me to tell you?"

"Yes, just say it."

"Okay, chill. We're going bowling."

"I haven't been to a bowling arena."

"Seriously? Wow, I'm taking you places you haven't been before." Technically, he's right. He's taken me on so many nice dates that I wouldn't have thought of myself.

As we drove to the place, we are listening to Fireboy DML & Asake. We kept singing the chorus of their songs. Their music was a vibe; we listened to it on repeat. When Teddy loved a song, he had to repeat it at least twice. We arrived at the bowling alley. I was so happy that I opened the door and ran out.

"Babe, where you are going?"

"I'm just so excited I felt like running to the door."

He's just shaking his head at me. We go to the counter and pay for entry into the bowling alley. We got our bowling shoes too. We walked over to our section and put our names on the board. At first when I was bowling, I was losing because my ball kept falling in the gutter. Jeremy was an experienced bowler. He felt bad for me.

The whole time, he kept saying, "You'll get it next time."

I had confidence in myself that I would at least hit the pins. After a while, I got the hang of it. Jeremy and I were tied at the end of the game. I was proud of myself because I didn't need gutter blockers. We agreed that it would be fun if we invited our friends next time.

Time passed and we were growing hungry. We ordered food. I got chicken wings with loaded tots and Minute Maid lemonade. Jeremy got extreme nachos with tater tots and Sprite. Both of us thought our food tasted great. Jeremy asked me how the party went last night.

Uh-oh! He wanted to know what happened. Well, people were drinking which wasn't that much of a shock to me. Only because it was to be expected in college. People underage drank all the time. McKenzie and Blake drank and were kind of buzzed. Jeremy told me that he didn't drink either because he didn't want to get caught one day by campus police.

"They are lucky that they had you and Rochelle helping them."

I mean there was some truth to it, but I didn't mind. "There were guys wanting to dance with Rochelle and me."

He immediately got jealous and said, "See, I knew you would tell me that. That's why I should've been there."

I was laughing, which made him ask why. I said, "You're acting jealous, and I've never seen that side of you." He tried to play it off like he wasn't, but we both knew. "Have you ever been to an off-campus party?"

"Actually I have, but that was last school year." Jeremy wasn't the party type, so I was intrigued. "It doesn't interest me. I've had my share of experiences going to one. Now I would only go if you went, to accompany you."

"What happened to make you stop partying? Also, I'd love to go to a party with you, babe."

"I'll tell you the reason to let you know the dangers of partying. If you're not careful, this can happen. There was a time where my friend Greg got so drunk that he got lost and my friends and I couldn't find him for an hour."

"Aye, really? What happened to him? Was he safe?"

"Turns out he walked to the local park and was sitting on the bench. Everyone was mad because we thought that something happened to him."

"That's not good, what he did. Anything could've happened to him."

"Tell me about it. After that, I was scared. It's not the half of it. He was put on academic probation and then got kicked out due to his poor academic performance. I haven't heard from him since."

Before I knew it, we were talking about how drinking could ruin your life if you weren't careful. Sometimes people became so dependent and used them as a crutch.

We decided after our conversation to head back to the dorm and watch a movie. On our way to campus, we listened to more tunes. Of course, being the passenger queen, I had to take over the aux cord and play my favorite music. I played a song by Gyakie, and it took us to another state mentally. You couldn't tell us nothing, that song was lit. We reached the campus dorm so fast. We walked to the dorm and then went to his room to get his laptop and HDMI cord. We ran downstairs into the main lounge, and it was empty. Jeremy set up the computer to the TV. He put on Netflix. We were debating on what movie to watch. We finally settled on *Next Friday*. It's the movie about Craig going to his cousin Day Day's house and his day spent over there. It was so funny, I couldn't contain my laughter. In one of the scenes, an African customer comes to the record store where Day Day works, acting all irate.

He said, "I can't get jiggy with this," in an African accent. He pulled out a CD that was broken and tried to return it. Then Craig came in and pushed the guy out. It was so ridiculously funny.

Jeremy and I couldn't contain our laughter. The movie was very entertaining. After that, we watched a TV show called *Raising Dion*. The show was alright, but I really couldn't get into it. I enjoyed my day so much and had to let Jeremy know. He was special to me and I cared so much about him. I knew the feelings were reciprocated, which was a great feeling. It was getting late, and Jeremy was getting tired. We called it a night and went to our dorm rooms. I tried to fall asleep but couldn't sleep for long. I wondered what was going on with me. For a while, I'd been trying my hardest to sleep, but my body wouldn't let me. It's like my brain was overstimulated, making it difficult. I hoped that I could get help when I was at counseling, or perhaps I could get melatonin from the store. Usually, I was weird about taking medication without seeking professional advice about my symptoms.

When it was morning, I felt so groggy and tired. I watched some *Kenan and Kel* on Netflix. That show was funny and put me in a good mood as well. I watched the show until about 1 pm. I was growing hungry, which was rare these days. I had the bright idea to cook one of my favorite meals that my mom made, corn-beef stew. I called Jeremy and asked him if he could take me to Walmart. It took some bribing to get him to say yes. I told him I'd make him some food. He was so filled with joy. We met up and he drove me to Walmart.

As I entered Walmart, I was overwhelmed by all the stuff in there. I know I'd been there before, but for some reason, I kept getting distracted. I told Jeremy to watch me and make sure I didn't overspend. Ingredients needed for the stew included corned beef, tomato sauce, tomatoes, large onion, oil, Maggi cubes, butter, salt, and a bell pepper. I grabbed jasmine rice to complete the meal. I tried to find a habanero or scotch bonnet pepper but was unable to find it. I realized that I needed pots and pans as well. I also got some cooking utensils. Then I picked up dishwashing soap, food storage containers, and a sponge.

When I went to the cashiers to pay for it, Jeremy stopped me and said, "Babe, I got this."

I tried to fight with him, but he wasn't budging. I caved in and let him pay because I didn't want to cause a scene. I thought it was a nice gesture. He drove us back to the dorm and helped me carry the groceries. We went to the basement kitchen to cook. No one is in the basement, so it was the perfect opportunity to cook. Jeremy washed the pot that we'd use while I cleaned the food and prepped it.

I called my mom to help me make this dish. First, she said to cut up onions and put it with oil in a pot. After that cooked, I put in tomato sauce and cut up tomatoes. While that cooked, I needed to add one Maggi bouillon cube. Then I added some cut up green bell pepper and let it cook before adding in the corn beef. Following my mom's instructions, the stew came out perfect, just how she would make it. I knew how to cook rice so that wasn't a big deal. Once the meal was finished, I made a plate for Jeremy and had him try.

He said, "Babe this is so delicious."

"I feel grateful that you like my cooking. My mom taught me good."

I was so happy because it was my first time making it. I tried it as well and had the same reaction. I put on my happy dance; nobody could tell me nothing. I'm a whole chef in these streets.

Jeremy helped me package the food into the containers. I gave him some to eat during the week and packed some food for myself. It was a good thing that I had a mini fridge. Jeremy was so excited that I cooked for him. He told me next time he would be cooking a dish from Trinidad.

"I'm waiting for that day," I told him.

We talked about other things and then it was time for us to leave because I noticed someone was waiting to use the kitchen. Jeremy helped take the equipment to my room. We decided to store the boxes under my bed. Jeremy gave me a hug and a kiss before heading out the door. A moment later Melissa came back in the room and asked what I did today. I told her I went to Walmart and cooked corn beef stew and rice with Jeremy.

She was like, "Wow! You're being a chef today."

I laughed. If it wasn't for my mom's help, I wouldn't have been able to make it. She said the next time I cooked, I should let her know. I would think about it 'cause we just got on talking terms. I told her sure just to keep the peace between us. I watched some TV shows until I got the idea to call Veronica. The last I heard, she was going on a date that I assumed was on Friday or Saturday.

I FaceTimed Veronica and she answered.

"Girl, I have something to tell you."

"What?" I ask in excitement.

"Aiden took me out on a date yesterday. We went to the Brooklyn Botanic Garden and saw tons of flowers and my favorite was the shrub rose. We walked through the Japanese garden and saw Japanese cherry blossoms. I wanted him to kiss me and hold my hand in the beginning, but we aren't together so that couldn't happen."

"In time, your wish will become a reality. As long as the vibes are right, and you both like one another, that's all that matters."

"It gets better. We went to Ogliastro pizza bar. I ordered pepperoni pizza and a lemonade. While he got a salsiccia which included tomato, sausages, and olives with a coke on the side. We both ate tiramisu della casa for dessert. We talked a lot and each time I spoke, he was interested in what I had to say. We kissed and it felt great to be honest, and not forced either." When she told me they kissed, I nearly fell off my bed.

I was like, "WOW!" She finally got what she's always wanted.

"Love your reaction girl. It literally caught me off guard, but it was a nice moment we shared. Here's the best part! He asked me to go on another date."

I was so thrilled when I heard that.

Then Veronica said, "What if he doesn't ask me to be his girlfriend?"

"I believe that if this is meant to be, the moment won't pass you by. Believe that all things are working for your good."

She understood where I was coming from because all things worked out in the end. Veronica told me that she was doing well in school and that her parents were well. I made an effort to ask how her father was, and she said he was doing alright. We talked more about dating and how it could be stressful if it was with the wrong person. Veronica and I, we could talk for hours. That's my girl for real.

CHAPTER

Seven

The Diagnosis

"NO! NO! NO!" I YELL. "YOU CAN'T MAKE ME GO, DR. STEVENS. I'M FINE, I know I am."

"I don't think you are stable enough to go back to your daily living just yet." We all knew what that meant: I would be admitted to the psych ward. "From my observations, your behavior is erratic and not like the Afua I know. You have been saying you're homesick, but I think it's deeper than that."

"What makes you think I want to be hospitalized? Omg, my life is ruined."

"I know this isn't what you want to hear, but I'm here to help you. When you came in and spoke, I noticed that you weren't present, like something was troubling you. Another thing I noticed was you took too long to respond to me, as if your mind was else-where, captivated by your thoughts."

108

"I have been going through a lot these past few weeks. Between being homesick and my mood swings causing my lack of sleep. I practically don't know what to do. I thought you would suggest I take melatonin. But you're telling me to be hospitalized. I trusted you."

Everything in me wanted to respond normally, but I was far deep into my illness which I would later come to know as bipolar disorder and depression. Those two married together were the worst feeling in my life. The person I knew was no longer there. I felt empty and the more I tried, the world came crashing down on me.

"Afua, are you alright?"

I didn't answer her. It was too late, the jig was up. Everything I had been fighting for the past few weeks came out and manifested itself into a mental breakdown. She said that if I didn't go, she would report me to the school. The college would then decide if I was mentally fit to stay in school. I was broken inside.

I felt betrayed by her. I began to cry profusely. I couldn't believe this was happening to me. Before I knew it, I was in the ambulance going to the nearest hospital. I couldn't really recall much of what happened. All I knew was I was in the hospital soon after and was placed in this waiting room with a TV inside. There was barely anyone. I was called into another room and asked some questions about school and why I thought I was brought to the hospital. There were security guards guarding the facility. They brought me to an empty room and told me to take off my clothes, including my accessories, and change into clothes handed to me. I also had to give them my shoes. I went back into the waiting room. Soon after they gave me medication to take, although I didn't know what it was. All I did was take the medication and didn't fight them on the situation. When I took the medication, somehow, I felt the same. Perhaps it hadn't kicked in yet. I stayed there for what felt like hours until someone asked me if I wanted something to eat. I declined because I wasn't hungry.

A while after, another staff member came and took me upstairs. I was sitting in a chair near the nurses' station for what felt like an eternity. I would see people passing by. My mind was contorted. Fading in and out of reality as time went by. Then I got up and someone was behind me, saying they would show me to my room. I walked slowly so the person could catch up to me. They showed me to a big and empty room. There was a toilet and sink inside. There I saw another woman named Emma, which I found out later. She was already sleeping in her bed. I saw my bed was made for me and they told me to lay down and get some rest. I don't know what was in that medication, but I eventually fell asleep. The first two days being in that facility was a blur.

Each time I tried to speak, I was not able to. My roommate would ask me if I was okay and I wouldn't say anything. That was unlike me, since I would've responded. I realized quickly that I wasn't myself. On the third day, I felt like myself again. I decided to call my mom and tell her where I was. I somehow remembered her number. I asked one of the staff members, Mr. Carter, how to use the phone. He was shocked that I spoke since I was mute for the last two days. He said dial nine, one, and then the number you wanted. If not, it would call someplace in the hospital. I thanked him then went on to use the phone. I dialed my mother's number.

She answered and asked, "Who is this?"

"It's me, Afua."

"Why are you calling me from a different number?"

That's when I broke down and told her I was in a psych ward.

She started screaming, "Jesus!" and crying. "My daughter, what happened to you?"

"I haven't been feeling like myself, Mommy. One day I went to my therapy session and my counselor said I wasn't acting like my normal self. That's when she called the ambulance." My mom was in shock; she thought I was alright.

"You keep me updated on your progress. One of these days, I will call off from work and drive down with your father."

I knew that when she told my dad it wasn't going to end well. I was very nervous. I told my mom I had to go because someone was waiting for the phone. She prayed for me and then said goodbye.

I was in a place where I didn't know anyone. I felt more alone than ever. To top it all off, my boyfriend didn't know I was there. I bet he was worried that he hadn't heard from me in two days. I would call him when I got the chance. I went back to my room and said hi to my roommate.

"Wow, you finally spoke to me."

"Ha-ha-ha, I'm so sorry about that. The medicine made me loopy for the past two days."

"I was worried thinking you didn't like me. Those medicines are very strong."

"Yeah, they are. Anyways, where are you from?"

"I'm originally from the city of Albany. This is my second time being admitted and I've already been here for a week."

"That's nice. Oh no, you've been here for a week? I hope you can get out soon then."

"I hope so too. Where are you from?"

"I'm from Brooklyn."

"I always wanted to visit New York City, but never had the chance."

"I think you should because there's so much to do in the city."

Mr. Carter knocked on the door and interrupted mid-sentence. He said, "Girls, it's time for lunch."

During this time, we collected our medication to take before lunch. Emma and I walked to the setting where people ate. I saw a bunch of people coming to the eating area. One of the staff members brought up the food to the unit. Today we were having lasagna with some veggies, banana bread, and juice. I waited for the crowd to go into the sitting area before entering. When the people crowded the place, my heart ached, causing my chest to tighten. My mind was overstimulated. I went in and found a place to sit, and Emma followed suit. I sat down and waited for my name to be called. One of the staff members passed me my food. The food was decent for being in a hospital, but I still disliked it. I forced myself to eat as much as I could. After I was finished, I stayed in the sitting area for a little while. Then I got called to speak to my doctor.

The doctor introduced herself to me and said her name was Dr. Monroe. "How are you feeling?"

All I said was, "Fine."

I would like to mention that during this time I was in the hallway of her office. I didn't like that other patients could hear my business. "I have a question about my diagnosis."

"Feel free to ask me."

"What is my diagnosis exactly?"

"You have bipolar disorder and depression."

I looked at her for a second and said, "That's not true. How come I'm given this diagnosis? I know I was depressed, but bipolar how?"

"Calm down, Afua. According to the hospital staff and my observations, you had a manic episode. You had a mental breakdown."

I didn't know how to react.

After that I didn't ask her anymore questions because it all made sense. The erratic behavior I was displaying was bipolar disorder. I went to a party, something I never did. I had this natural high all the time until recently.

"Well, if you ever need me, do not hesitate to ask the staff members."

"Thank you." I went to the pay phone to call Jeremy. Someone was using the phone, so I waited my turn.

Finally, it was my turn. I dialed Jeremy's number and I was so nervous. All these thoughts came to mind. I kept thinking he'd call me crazy and want nothing to do with me.

He answered the phone and said, "Hello, who is this?"

"Hey, it's Afua."

He stopped talking for a minute and we were just in silence. "Babe, I've been wondering, what happened to you? Your roommate texted me on Instagram saying she hasn't seen you in two days. I even tried to call your number, and you didn't answer. Please tell me you're alright."

"I am not okay. I'm in the psych ward."

He lost it. He began to cry and that's something I hadn't seen him do. "I'm so sorry that you're there by yourself. I wish you didn't have to go through this alone."

"Do you love me despite this?" I said with a strained voice, holding back tears.

He recited a Bible verse from 1 Corinthians 13:4-8. It read, "'Love is patient, love is kind. It does not envy, it does not boast, it is not proud. It does not dishonor others, it is not self-seeking, it is not easily angered, it keeps no records of wrongs. Love does not delight in evil but rejoices with the truth. It always protects, always trusts, always hopes, always perseveres. Love never fails.'

"I will fight for our relationship no matter the cost. You shouldn't feel bad because remember, I have a family member who has a mental illness and see all that they go through. I pray you find healing and that God guides and protects you during your stay. May you keep God close to you and be surrounded with caring staff. In Jesus' name we pray, amen. I will try to find a way out of work to see you okay, my love? I will also find out what unit you're on and look up the visiting hours. You are never alone when you have me."

"Okay, thanks so much, babe." I began crying, unable to hold back my tears. I wanted to be back on campus. Oh, how I wished I could see his face right now. I could only imagine how he felt right now. The more I thought about it, tears started to flow from my eyes.

"Everything will be alright, Afua. Do not cry. Talk to you later."

"Talk to you later." That phone call made me feel like I was in prison. I was mad that I didn't ask my doctor how long I'd be here. I walked back to my room when I heard from the staff that we would be having art therapy time. I walked into the classroom and was greeted by a woman whose name was Mrs. Looney. I noticed that only two other people decided to participate in this therapy session. Mrs. Looney introduced herself to us and told us we would be listening to music and drawing. The fun part was that we get to pick the song one after another. Then we would draw how the music made us feel. I chose the new song by Kidi called "Champagne." I heard this song one day and it was all good vibes. The song made me think of flowers and the beautiful sky. I couldn't wait for the day I got my freedom. It reminded me of the Lisa "Left Eye" Lopes documentary when she talked about being in the diversion center. She was given time outside for a few hours and she was marveling at how beautiful outside was after being inside for so long.

The other person played Leone Bridges' "Coming Home" while the another played Mariah Carey's "Fantasy." Mrs. Looney thanked us for participating in the activity and said we were welcome to leave. Before I left, I asked her if I could take out a book. She said I could as long as I filled out the sheet with my name. I checked out the popular self-help book *You are a Badass* by Jen Sincero. I was excited I found this book since someone suggested it to me. I thanked Mrs. Looney and headed out the door. I walked back to my room and my roommate is there. I asked her why she didn't participate in art therapy. She told me that she didn't feel like it and that it wasn't mandatory. Reading my book didn't change the fact that the time was standing still. It's as if the minutes were dragging by. I was growing bored of this place already. There were not enough things to do here besides watch a community TV. I had to find something to do to keep me sane. I walked to the nurse station and asked for a pen and notebook.

Nurse Eliana looked at me and said, "I will see if we have those available. I'll give them to you in a few minutes."

I walked back to my room, eager to write my feelings down and make sense of my current state of emotions. Minutes passed and Nurse Eliana came by my room with supplies in hand, ready to give them to me.

She said, "I hope you can make use of these."

I was so grateful for the pen and notebook. I expressed my appreciation to her before beginning to write. The words just flowed from my mind. I began writing.

I'd never be the same. My life had taken an infinite turn. When I looked at my life, I used to see darkness sometimes. I was succumbed by my fears and depression took over me. No matter what I did, I couldn't find solace. Then I met you. You made me glow and for a second, all my stress was carried away. My life had light, but nothing could change the issues I lived with inside. Tears rolled from my eyes onto my pillow. As I cried, self-defeating thoughts came to mind. Would you love me when it hurts? When I push you away with my actions. When your words can't soothe my fractured heart. Would you dance with me in the rain? Through this difficult storm that was created in my mind. Would you look into my eyes and say, 'baby it's gonna be alright?' Did you know I lived with intrusive thoughts? They played over in my mind like a broken record skipping my favorite part. That's when I learned that this fight was not my own but that of the Lord. Life would disappoint and so would man, but the Lord's love endures forever. So, pick your head up and know that darkness never prevails for long. Where there's dullness, he illuminates. Where there is sorrow, he encourages.

It felt therapeutic, writing my thoughts down. Time passed and it was time for us to eat dinner. I felt like not too long ago we were just eating lunch. I went to the sitting area and waited for my name to be called. We were having meatloaf and mashed potatoes with a fruit cocktail. I wasn't thrilled about our food selection. I ate what I could and threw the rest out. A girl named Isabella came to me and introduced herself. She asked me how I liked the food, and I told her it was okay but not to my liking. I thought that the conversation was weird, but I didn't question it. I went into the TV room that was being supervised by the security guard. The news was playing which I found boring, so I left after a few minutes. I walked to my room and just laid on my bed. I thought about my life and how at this very moment I was a failure. I let myself and my family down.

How did this happen to me? I tried to be a good person. I wondered what I did to deserve this. My life would never be the same. Would I even be able to finish college, let alone pass my current classes? All these thoughts in my head. The more I thought about it the sadder I felt. I wanted to cry but I couldn't. If I cried so much, they might keep me here longer than expected. I had to play my cards right so that I could leave. I was not going to make a spectacle of myself in this place. Doing my best to think positive, nothing could change my mood. Soon I was informed that the shower was open for anyone who needed to take a shower. I went because I hadn't showered in a while and wanted to smell fresh. I told the staff member to write my name down for shower time. I needed change of clothes, and they said they would have scrubs available for me to change into. In that moment, I realized that I probably should call Jeremy and ask him to bring me clothes tomorrow. My name wouldn't be called for a while, so I used the opportunity to call him.

I dialed his number and he answered. "Hey, if you can this week, is it possible for you to bring me some clothes?"

"Tomorrow I'll stop by your dorm and collect some of your clothes and bring them to you during visiting hours."

"Thank you, and I appreciate what you're doing for me."

"You are most certainly welcome." Before I know it, my name is being called. I ran to the staff member standing by the shower room.

Mrs. Brooks asked me if I would like a towel, toothbrush, toothpaste, shower gel, body lotion, deodorant, and makeshift flip flops. I told her I would like all of them.

I asked her, "Can I have some clothes?"

She gave me some scrubs.

I went into the shower and it was pretty small and creepy in there. I got in the shower and the water was coming fast and hard. I quickly washed my body and headed out. The shower made me feel better. I walked back to my room and just laid down for the meantime. Mrs. Davis, who has short dreadlocks and glasses, walked into the room. She had a nice demeanor about her, like a loving parent. She introduced herself to me because I was new, and she hadn't seen me before today. She asked Emma and I if we are alright. We both replied with yes.

I asked her for more things to read and she said, "I can get you a Bible if that works for you."

"Yes, that works. And can I have some shoes?" I was barefoot and the floor was cold against my feet.

She told us if we needed anything else, to just let her know. I said thank you and she left the room. I knew I had another book that I was currently reading but I liked to have options. A few minutes later Mrs. Davis came back with a Bible and what appeared to be water shoes. She handed them to me, and I said thank you. She had this energy about her that was captivating. She left and I tried on my shoes. They were orange and looked so beautiful. I appreciated the little things in life. The fact that she brought me shoes was amazing. I opened the Bible and stumbled across Romans 8:28 which said, "And we know that in all things God works for the good of those who love him, who have been called according to his purpose." This gave me hope that my situation would get better. God worked in mysterious ways. Perhaps this experience was a testimony for me to tell others. Whatever the reason was, reading the Bible made me more at ease. A moment later, a staff member came and told us it was snack time. We just ate before, why do we need snacks? I went anyway and waited in the sitting area.

Mr. Carter was pushing a cart. He asked me if I would like apple or cranberry juice. I took the cranberry juice. They had three types of sandwiches today. There were cheese, turkey and cheese, and peanut butter and jelly sandwiches. He passed me a peanut butter and jelly sandwich since I had no preference for what to eat.

I talked to Emma and told her that at this rate I'd gain ten pounds.

She said, "Yeah, they feed us well here."

After our snack I went back to our room and just tried to get some sleep. I eventually fell asleep.

I woke up the next morning well-rested for the first time in weeks. I brushed my teeth and got myself looking as presentable as I could. I went into the TV room and saw that a few people were up, but my roommate was still asleep. I sat down and watched the news, but as usual, I got bored. The security guard was sitting there, and started a conversation with me.

"My name is Mr. Young. What's your name?"

"My name is Afua."

"That's a beautiful name."

"Thank you. So where are you from?"

"I am from Belize. What about you?"

"My parents are from Ghana."

"That's amazing. Always wanted to go ever since the year of the return."

Here's a little back story. In 2019, people traveled as a destination spot. This was when people went to Ghana to discover or trace their ancestry. "It is never too late to travel. Ghana is going beyond the return to promote tourism and build connections between African countries."

"That is very true. I must say, I am surprised you're talking to me. When you first came in, you weren't the best mentally."

"I know, I was mentally checked out."

"Do you remember anything from those days?"

"Nope, everything is a blur."

"I am very delighted that you're doing well."

We talked for a while, until another staff member announced it was breakfast time. By that time everyone was up and walking around. The staff members woke up the ones that weren't.

I walked into the sitting area and the staff members were passing out coffee and tea. I asked for tea because I wasn't a coffee type of person. I put some milk and sugar into mine just like my mom used to at home. After that they passed us our food. Today for breakfast, we were eating French toast with syrup and a fruit cup. I was thinking about Jeremy coming to visit me and how exciting that would be. Emma asked me what had me daydreaming and I told her I had a visitor coming. She asked a follow up question about the person that was coming. I told her it was my boyfriend.

She said, "Wow! That is nice, it shows that he cares. Some people, regardless of how long you've been together, once they hear mental illness, they leave. They think you're crazy and need help."

I was initially afraid that he would leave me at my lowest moment, but he was showing me otherwise. I appreciated him for seeing me the way I always wanted. Since the day I met him, he's been so kind and patient with me. Talking about him made me emotional. After I finished eating, I asked the nurses at the station when the doctor would be on the unit. They said during lunch time. One of the nurses called me over to get my vital signs for blood pressure done. After that, I went back to my room and read the book *You are a Badass*. The author was dropping some serious gems. I found the book fascinating.

After that I grabbed my notebook and pencil to write down my sentiments. This is what I came up with.

Isn't it funny how life changes? You could be at the height of your life and it could all come tumbling down. The spark that once captivated souls now diminished. You look at yourself thinking, when will this period in my life stop? Only to find that it was a constant cycle of struggle and pain so deep you suffer in silence. The moment you realized others could see your agony too is when embarrassment filled your heart. You wanted an escape but those intrusive thoughts kept you awake at night. Haunted by those memories of how life should've been. You sought help but things never changed. So the cycle repeated until one day you exploded into a myriad of your own reflection. Your essence was lost, but don't fret; life gets better. It might take some time, and surely you'll doubt yourself, but don't give up. The world in its entirety needs you.

An hour passed by, and Emma asked me if I wanted to play Jenga with her. I agreed because I hadn't played Jenga in a long time and I thought it would be fun. We walked to the nurses' station and ask them for the Jenga set. One of them gave it to Emma and we went into the TV room to play. Emma laid down the blocks and then stacked them up. We began playing. I was so focused because I wanted to win. We both took out the blocks carefully as we went along. I saw Isabella coming towards the table and sit close to observe us playing. Emma got distracted and the Jenga blocks came tumbling down. I won that first round, which made me happy. Then Isabella interrupted our game to asks us how the food was from breakfast. We said it was alright.

Then she asked us, "How we are enjoying our stay?"

Enjoying? How can we enjoy ourselves in a psych ward. This was just something that we had to do to get better. There's nothing fun about this. What she meant to say was, 'how are you doing,' but I digress. I just said things weren't bad, but they certainly weren't the best. She wanted to know why I said that. It's because I didn't expect to be here, I was forced. So being here wasn't the best thing in the world. The whole time, I just wanted to go back to playing my game.

She said, "Oh I get it, but none of us wanted to be here either." Then she walked off. Emma and I looked at each other, shocked.

Then Emma said, "Don't mind her, she's weird. Every new person she sees, she wants to badger them with questions."

I said, "Ah! I understand." And continued playing Jenga. We played six rounds in total and ended up tied in the end.

Time flies by fast when you're occupied. It was time for lunch. We lined up to get into the sitting room. We got inside and sat down. Emma and I talked about what we would be eating. One of the staff told us that we would have burgers and fries. I was full of excitement when I heard that. I waited for my name to be called and then got my food. I ate it and felt satisfied. Both Emma and I talked about how we liked the food selection today. After I finished eating, I asked Mr. Carter when visiting hours were. He told me that it was from 2-6 pm. I looked at the clock and saw it was almost time. I realized that Teddy would see me looking like this.

"Oh my gosh!" Well, at least I'd get to see him. I went into my room and anticipated them calling me for visiting hours. In the meantime, I just laid in my bed thinking about school and how I'd make up the work. Thirty minutes passed by and I got a knock on my door telling me that I had a visitor. I quickly got up and began singing to myself because I would be seeing Jeremy. I walked to the sitting area and saw that he was sitting there. As soon as he saw me, he got up. I couldn't see his facial expression because he was wearing a mask. His eyes sparkled. He came to hug me. I felt so loved by him.

He said, "Babe, how are you doing?"

I told him that I was hanging in there and I was able to make use of my time. As I told him this, tears started to form in his eyes. I had never seen him this emotional. As I held his hand, I told him he didn't need to cry. He told me that he hated seeing people in the hospital. He wished this never happened to me.

"I'm glad you're here," I said.

I go on to say that normally mental illness got a bad rep. As soon as someone found out that you had a mental illness, they felt like they'd have to babysit and monitor you or they wanted to save you from yourself. They left you when you needed them the most because they weren't ready for such responsibility. They didn't realize that it wasn't their job to save you. Jeremy looked me in my eyes and told me that he would never think of leaving me. Everyone had their struggles, and it didn't mean you were any less because of it. He kept saying how happy he was to see me.

He handed me some of my things and told me that my roommate was worried about me. She asked him questions, but he didn't think it was appropriate to tell her my problems. "I just told her that you are alright and safe."

I appreciated that so much, which made me emotional. Jeremy respected my privacy. I was quite vulnerable. I would let people know when I was ready.

"Babe, I want to take away your pain. I know you've been struggling with depression, but you're not in this alone. I will continue to nurture you and our relationship."

Why did I have the sweetest man in the world? I valued Jeremy so much. Since our encounter he's always shown me how a woman was supposed to be treated. I hated having people see me under these conditions. My eyes began to water as I fought back tears. Jeremy told me that it was okay to cry because these weren't the best circumstances.

He held my hand and told me that I was the rose that grew from concrete, proving everyone wrong. I remembered hearing this poem by Tupac Shakur and how it was beautifully written. That was the first time I ever heard anyone refer to me as resilient in that way. He said I learned to beat all the odds stacked against me. I would one day be able to tell my story as a testament of what God could do. I was encouraged by his words. He couldn't stay long because visiting hours were about to end. He gave me a hug and told me to hang in there and I would be out soon. Jeremy said he would revisit next week or sooner if I needed to see him. He gave me a big hug. We embraced each other for as long as we could before he finally left. I walked him to the exit even though the security guard was standing near the door. I wished him safe travels. I walked back to my room with blurred-teary eyes. There was a heaviness in my chest as I walked back. My roommate was there, and she asked me why I was sad.

"Girl, why are you sad? You had a visitor, which is more than what most people get here. That means the person cares about you."

Although she was right, my mind wouldn't let me be happy. Here I was in this place, stuck for Lord knows how long. I thought it was the fact that I didn't have freedom here. "You are right, I should be grateful. It was just the whole interaction with my boyfriend left me vulnerable."

"It's okay, you'll be alright. This isn't forever, you know. Soon you'll be out and not confined to this place, just try to keep the hope alive."

I just laid in my bed, thinking about when I'd be able to leave when I got a knock on the door. It was Dr. Monroe, and she asked to speak with me in the hallway. I wondered why she couldn't tell me in the room. I walked to the hallway, and she told me that she had good news for me.

"You will be leaving next Friday. You've made some good improvement with your medication." The sensations in my chest went away and turned into a grin. "We'll keep you for a few more days to monitor your behavior, and once you're discharged, someone will give you a call about your outpatient care moving forward. Sounds good?"

"That is more than good, it's amazing news. Thank you for letting me know." I thought this would be a great opportunity to call my mom and tell her the news. I ran to the phone and called my parents.

This time my dad picked up and told me that he was happy to

hear from me. He said he already knew what happened to me. He was concerned about my wellbeing.

"Afua, I feel like I failed you. I'm sorry you're in the hospital."

"You didn't fail me, I was just going through a lot and didn't express myself to you. For that, I'm extremely sorry."

"You do not have to apologize. I should've been there more." I told him that the doctor said I would be out on Friday.

"I'm happy to hear that. Your mom and I will be staying in Albany from Wednesday to Friday. We will be visiting you during visiting hours."

I was filled with joy that my parents would be coming. It was good speaking to him, since I barely heard from him. We said our goodbyes before hanging up. I walked back to my room. Moments later, there was another knock on the door, signaling it was dinner time. I lined up as usual and waited for the staff to open the sitting room. I immediately found a place to sit and waited for my name to be called.

For today's dinner, we would be having beef Bolognese with a bread roll and juice. Emma and I talk about my visit with Jeremy.

"Girl, what happened with your boyfriend?"

"It was good seeing him, but it got emotional. I wanted to be released today just so I could have more time with him. It made me realize how little freedom we have being in here. He did offer words of encouragement to me. It made me sad once he left, but in the same breath, it was refreshing to see him."

"Wow, that man really loves you, because not many people would stay in a relationship with someone in our condition."

Her words had me thinking about how lucky I was. In Ghana there's a saying, "Ɔdɔ kɔ baabi a ɔdɔ wɔ,"which means love goes where love is. You should go where you were appreciated and cared for. Never stay in a situation that's not bearing fruit. The love that Jeremy had for me was genuine. I just hoped I wasn't wrong in my feelings. I finished eating my food and went to throw away the garbage. I got told by another staff member, Mrs. Wilson, that they would be watching Beyoncé's *Black is King* in the classroom. She asked me if I wanted to watch it.

I said, "Yes of course, anything is better than doing nothing in my room."

I went over to the classroom and washed my hands because we were still practicing good hygiene. I waited for people to come into the room. One of the people that came in happened to be my roommate, and behind her was Isabella. Emma walked over and sat next to me, and Isabella followed suit. Isabella tried to talk to me, acting like she didn't have an attitude with me earlier.

I let it go because one thing I didn't need was an enemy during my stay. I was lowkey giving her the side eye,' cause why are you behaving like nothing ever happened. Then I remembered what Emma said about her and realized maybe she had some personality issue or something. But it wasn't my place to diagnose her. As I watched *Black is King*, I was vibing with the music and it captivated my soul. I even saw Shatta Wale in the film with Beyoncé. I was so elated when I saw my fellow Ghanaian alongside Beyoncé. I was singing along. I enjoyed myself the whole time. The influence of African culture made me really love the film. After it was done, I was quite sad because I wanted to watch more. I walked towards my room when they announced it was snack time. I got my snack, ate it, and left quickly because I wanted to hurry and take a shower. I asked to take a shower and got my clothes ready. When my name was called, I went into the shower. Always felt creeped out by the shower, but I'd rather shower than smell. Once I finished, I headed to bed immediately. I was so tired I fell asleep. Fast forward a few days and I felt better than ever mentally. Jeremy came to visit me again and it was really nice seeing him. He assured me that I would be alright as long as I kept God first in all I did. He was happy that I was leaving on Friday. I woke up in a great mood. I remembered what my parents told me about staying in Albany for the next three days. Today was Wednesday, so I was expecting them to come and visit me. Every day I woke up, it was a reminder that I was closer to my release date.

Breakfast and lunch were good. We had a cheese omelet with hashbrowns and juice for breakfast, and for lunch, we had chicken noodle soup with a bread roll and juice. I spent the rest of my time anticipating my parents' arrival. As I laid on my bed, I kept replaying in my mind what would happen. Possibly my parents would think I was unfit to remain on campus. I really wanted to be on campus, I worked too hard to let my efforts all come tumbling down. They would try to tell me it was because I didn't pray enough, and this was the result. Oh gosh, I could feel my stomach fluttering and my hands trembling. I was so nervous for my parents to see me there like that. Granted I was feeling much better, however, them seeing me in this environment was a bit embarrassing. It made me appear like a failure. I went to school in hopes of making them proud, only to be in a psych ward. All of a sudden, my eyes were tearing up. To distract myself, I started to read. I was reading and the book mentioned that it wasn't your fault if your life was messed up, but it became your fault if you stayed down in that mess. It reminded me of my situation. I shouldn't let it define me. After some time passed, I got a knock on my door saying I had visitors waiting for me. My heart stopped for a second and nervousness filled my body. I walked to the sitting room and saw my mom and dad by the table. They each gave me a hug.

"We are happy to see you," my mom said.

"Thank you, Mommy and Daddy. I'm grateful to the both of you for taking off work to see me."

My mom said, "Afua, you're our child we'll do anything just to see you happy and healthy. Don't think for a second we don't care about you."

My dad asked, "How are you doing so far?"

"I'm pretty much okay. I try to keep myself busy for the most part."

He said, "Well that's good you're keeping your mind occupied."

"I have to tell you that I had a visitor not too long ago." Both of them were curious as to who the visitor was. I was reluctant to tell them since my dad would overreact and lecture me.

My mom said, "My daughter, it's okay, just tell us who it was."

I thought about it for a second. Finally, I blurted. "My boyfriend came to see me."

My dad said, "Aye, so you have a boyfriend already in school? I hope he isn't distracting you."

"No, he isn't, and he's a really good guy. I wouldn't be with someone that would bring disgrace to myself. He brought me clothes when I didn't have any while being here."

"He's good for doing that for you. I would like to thank him at some point," my mom said.

"Actually, he is planning on seeing me when I leave the hospital. You can meet him then."

My parents and I talked about what my plans were after leaving the hospital Friday. I told them that I planned on staying in college and finishing the semester. My parents expressed their reservations about me wanting to stay. They wanted me to come home and transfer to a school in NYC. Ultimately, I felt defeated. Unheard. After all it was my life and being in college hadn't been all bad. I met amazing people. This wasn't the end of my story, just the beginning. I told my parents that my position on this matter still stood. I wanted to stay on campus and continue my college career there.

My mom said, "Well, we can't force you to do something your heart isn't into. All I want is for you to be happy in life."

Then my dad said, "To be frank, I'm not overzealous with your decision, but I understand why you want to stay here. I too want what's best for you, Afua."

I took it all in, but I'd made my mind up already. After that, they were asking me about the food and how I liked it, and I said the food was alright. As long as I was fed, that's all that mattered. They stayed for a while longer and were asking me how I like my roommate and being in that room. I told them that she was nice, and I liked being in my room for the most part.

Before they left, my mom said something that would stick with me. She said, "Ka w'akoma to wo yam and Nya gyidie na bɔmpae." This translated to, don't worry; have faith and pray.

I was sad to see them leave but I was happy I'd see them the next day. The rest of the night and the next day was a blur to me, going by so fast. Before I knew it, it was Friday—the day I was patiently awaiting. I woke up super early and was talking to the security guard, Mr. Young. I told him that today I was leaving. He was distraught that I was leaving. He asked me what my plans were after my departure from this place. I told him I wanted to stay in college and finish the semester.

He said that was awesome and I should continue to do what was best for me. "Never give up, because this world will try to take your life away from, you but don't falter."

After our conversation was over, I took a shower, changed clothes, and brushed my teeth. I was told by my doctor that I could leave around 12 pm. For breakfast, I had pancakes and eggs with turkey bacon and juice. I called my parents and tell them to pick me up at 12, and told Jeremy that he could meet us by my dorm after. I went to my room and gathered the little stuff I had and made sure my side of the room was clean. I returned my book that I borrowed then went back to my room. I thanked Emma for being a good room-mate to me and told her how much I appreciated her kindness. She told me that she would miss me and that she'd also be leaving next week.

I was waiting for the clock to turn to 12 pm so I could sign the paperwork to be released. As soon as the time came, I went to the main desk and asked to check out. The nurse handed me some docu-ments to sign. She then handed me a bag with some personal care items and food. She also gave me a bag of my clothes that were washed. The staff told me goodbye and so did Emma. Before I left, she asked for my number so we could keep in contact. I left soon after. It became so surreal to me that I would be back to my daily life. The freedom felt so good. I took the elevator down to the main lobby.

I saw my mom and dad waiting for me. They gave me a hug and we walked out of the hospital. My dad drove me back to my dorm room. On the way to my dorm, I texted Jeremy to go to the main lobby to meet me and my parents. My parents and I walked to the dorm, and we saw him. He greeted my parents and introduced himself to them. Both of my parents thanked him for all he did for me and started saying they prayed he would continue to be a great person inside and out. They said they would like to take him out for lunch. I was really happy that my parents liked Jeremy, because they could be critical of people at times. We decided to get soul food and I was there for it. We went to a place called Sunday's Soul Food and the food was amazing. We ended up having their most popular plate which was called Sunday Dinner. It included fried chicken, cornbread, mac and cheese, and collard greens. It was a great time hanging out with my parents. We left feeling satisfied and filled with laughter. My dad drove us back to the dorm while they headed back to the hotel. They said tomorrow they'd head back to Brooklyn.

The Aftermath

"Afua, what happened to you? I was so worried when I didn't see you for days. I tried asking Jeremy, but he wouldn't tell me. Is everything alright?"

Melissa was concerned about me? That was really interesting, being that it was not too long ago that we got on speaking terms. Plus, she played hockey and hung out with Noah. I didn't think she would even notice I was gone. This showed that she had indeed changed.

"Well, if I'm going to tell you what happened, I need your undivided attention. This is something I do not want many people to know about just yet. I'm hoping you don't tell anyone this."

"I'm all ears, your story is safe with me."

"Well, I was at my counseling session when my therapist noticed something was wrong with me and said I needed to go to the hospital. Next thing I knew I'm admitted to the psych ward. It took me by surprise because I didn't expect to be in the hospital."

Tears welled in Melissa's eyes as I told her this story. "Afua, I'm so sorry that happened to you. How do you feel now?"

"I'm doing much better. I'm glad I got the help I needed because for a while I couldn't sleep well through the night. I didn't feel like myself. I will be receiving treatment moving forward from the outpatient center."

"That's good things are getting better for you. I believe that things are working in your favor despite this occurring. You are making progress forward towards the life you want." We had a deep conversation, and I felt that her demeanor towards me changed after that. I didn't know what it was, but I had this belief that everything would be alright between us. I was at peace with the current state of our relationship. It took us not seeing eye to eye for things to come together. This made our connection with each other much stronger than before. I decided to go to bed and watch my favorite show. It felt good for once to be in the comfort of my room. Since it hadn't been the best of times being at the hospital. Especially being monitored 24/7 by someone wasn't a great feeling. I fell asleep so fast, which was a surprise to me. Before I knew it, it was the next morning and I was receiving a call from my mom telling me to get dressed because we were having breakfast together. I ran to the bathroom, showered, and got ready for the morning with my parents. My dad came to pick me up. They asked me where I'd like to go, and I said IHOP.

We approach IHOP and I was so excited. As we entered the establishment, we were greeted by a man who brought us to our seats. He told us that our waiter would be with us momentarily. A few minutes later, a woman came and gave us the menu, which we quickly looked through. I decided on getting the chicken and pancakes with a blue raspberry lemonade splasher. My mom got the smokehouse combo with a wild berry lemonade splasher. My dad got the breakfast sampler with the mango lemonade splasher. My mom talked to me about how my life moving forward would change and that I should be prepared for it. In my mind I was thinking how she was right, but I was resilient so I could overcome anything. I told her that I understood, but my life would be fruitful regardless.

She agreed and then my dad chimed in and said, "So you still want to stay at college in Albany?"

"Yes, because it's not like me to give up when the going gets tough." They both said as long as I did what made me content, they'd support me. They were telling me how my siblings were so worried about me when they heard the news. I should get in contact with them since I hadn't heard from them. It had been a rollercoaster of emotions these past two weeks.

I totally forgot about them. I kind of felt embarrassed that they knew, but this was part of my journey. My siblings knowing didn't mean anything; they loved me regardless. We really had an intense conversation, which I didn't expect. The food was amazing and made me full. My parents decided to take me to Walmart after to get some food and personal care items for my dorm. I really valued my parents and was thankful for them. After shopping, we headed back to the dorm. They helped me take the stuff into my room. We prayed and my parents told me that God should remain number one in my life. They also told me that they would drive back to Brooklyn today and that if I needed anything they were just a call away.

I was filled with immense sorrow that they were leaving for some reason. I mean, I wanted to stay in school but here I was, experiencing all the emotions. I laid in my bed just thinking maybe I made a mistake. I couldn't let my parents think they were right, so I did what I normally did, which was suck it up and push through. I started to think of a plan of attack because moving forward I wanted to better my life in every aspect: physically, spiritually, emotionally, and mentally. I didn't want history to repeat itself with my mental health. I decided that I would be empowered by the situation. I called my bestie Veronica since I saw that I had a missed call from her during the time I was in the hospital.

I FaceTimed her and she immediately picked up and said, "Girl, I've been waiting on you to call me back. What happened?"

"I know, girl. I apologize for that. When you called, I was admitted to the psych ward and being diagnosed with bipolar disorder and depression."

She was so shocked. "I'm so sorry, Afua. How are you doing? Is there anything I can do?"

I was grateful for her just listening to me speak about my experience. She asked me what my plans were moving forward. I told her that I planned on staying in school and pushing through. I would also receive outpatient care from the hospital's mental health facility. Somehow, we ended up talking about relationships and dating. She told me that she's officially dating Aiden. He asked her to be his girlfriend fairly quick. I was very excited to hear that news. She began to say that he was treating her well and taking her out on nice dates. They went to a haunted house recently and it was fun. I thought about the pumpkin I had sitting in my room and how I didn't get to carve it with Jeremy. I figured it was too late because the month was almost over. While still talking to Veronica, I threw out the pumpkin, being that it appeared to be spoiled.

"How are things going with Jeremy?"

"It's great, he actually came to see me at the hospital. He also got to meet my parents, and they liked him although I know he was nervous."

She was so amazed and thrilled for me. Veronica knew what my parents were like. For them to like him showed he's a great guy. Two hours passed, and we were still catching up. We noticed that we were on the phone too long and decided to call it quits.

The next day was quite uneventful because nothing really happened, other than me watching TV shows. Then I came to the realization that I needed to do something with my time. I wrote down a list of things that I needed to do, such as reaching out to my professors to tell them what happened and if I could make up the work. Then I needed to reach out to my job and to Stacy to tell her that I would not be participating in the hair show.

Despite the fact my professors might not respond to my emails until Monday, I still emailed them. I figured that I would knock on Stacy's door and explain to her as well. As I approached her door, an overwhelming sense of nervousness filled my body. I knocked on her door and she opened it. She was pleased to see me.

"Is everything alright?" she asked.

"Yes, but I have to speak with you privately."

"Sure." She quickly set up a chair in her room for us to talk.

I sat and then started to apologize for not attending the modeling practices. She told me not to worry about it. I told her the reason she hadn't seen me. She was just speechless. She told me how sorry she was for not checking up on me.

Stacy then said that I should try to focus on myself and forget about modeling for the hair show. In her words, she said that now was the time for me to not overextend myself because freshman year set the trajectory of how my college life would be. Especially GPA-wise. Even though this hurt me hearing this, it made sense. I was trying to do a lot of things at once, forgetting that my mental health came first. So, I made a decision to not do the hair show. It was coming up and I would be unprepared, and I didn't like stressing myself. It was like a weight was lifted off my shoulders. I was grateful that she was so understanding. She asked me how I was feeling, and I said fine. After that we talked for a few, and then I was out the door. I laid in my bed thinking how my life was about to change because of this diagnosis. Life had a way of showing you what was important even when you're oblivious to it. The whole time I was putting energy to everything else instead of my mental health. Look what it got me. I ended up in the hospital. Now I was trying to recover from the whole ordeal because it was traumatizing. Despite this, I had to give myself grace because I did not know what I know now. If I want change to happen in my life, I had to be disciplined and work for it. If no one else was going to tell me, I would. I was capable of excelling in college.

The next day came, and I had a plan of action. All of my thoughts from yesterday kept flooding my mind. I understood that true change started with me. I was lost in thought when I received a ding on my phone. I checked it to find that my professors had responded to my email. I was really nervous to open the messages. What if they denied my request to make up work? Surely, they might say that my excuse isn't valid and want proof. To my surprise, they were all understanding because they understood that my situation was unexpected and tragic. They gave me until the end of the semester to finish my assignments. When I tell you I let out the biggest scream. God really was so good to me. Especially during this time when my life was shifted. It wasn't the easiest situation to deal with but I was glad that God helped until this point. I got ready to go to my job and speak with my supervisor. I walked to the library, hopeful that my supervisor would be understanding.

As soon as I entered the library, I got so much love from my coworkers. They asked me what happened because they hadn't seen me in a while. I told them that an emergency happened that I couldn't talk about in depth. They were so understanding, which touched my heart. I asked if my supervisor was in, and they said yes. I went behind the desk and went to the back office.

I saw my supervisor and she was shocked to see me.

She said, "Afua, where have you been? I was worried when you didn't come to work. Is everything alright?"

I explained to her what happened. As I did, I saw tears form in her eyes. She said she was so sorry and wanted to hug me. She wanted to take away my pain but that wasn't her job.

I was grateful to her for not judging me and being upset. I hated feeling sorry for myself. It didn't help me to wallow in self-pity. So, moving forward, I wasn't going to do that. After the conversation, I felt better. And to think my life changed and I was down about it. I walked to my room and sat down for a while. As I did, I got a knock on my door. It was Jeremy.

"Babe, what are you doing here?"

He smiled and said, "I know life has been difficult for you these past weeks and I wanted to cheer you up. I made you Pelau, which is a Trinidadian dish. It has stewed meat, rice, and veggies."

That wasn't all; he also brought me a drink called Sorrel. I thanked him and gave him the biggest hug. Words couldn't express how I was feeling. I wanted to cry but I didn't. I held back my tears.

"It was no hassle, I wanted to do something nice for you. I got the recipe from my mom." He took his time to make me something. It improved my mood.

He left shortly after and told me to enjoy my meal. I put on my favorite show and began eating. I had to say, he really did his thang with making this food. It was delicious and paired great with the drink. It was a great escape from the task at hand. I really had the best man ever.

After fifteen minutes passed, the door opened and it was Melissa. She was in a cheery mood which wasn't unusual, but either way, good for her. She greeted me and asked how I'm doing, and if everything worked out for me with adjusting back to my normal routine. I told her yes, everything was fine despite knowing there would be a lot of work for me to do. I was already overwhelmed. I'd keep pushing through because a girl like me never quit, even when things got tough. Somehow, we started talking about her dating life. She said things were going well with her and Noah. She was smiling so much because he just asked her to be his girlfriend. In my mind I thought about how she just got over heartbreak and already was in a new relationship like nothing happened. That's very interesting how she bounced back. I told her I was happy for her. She was so cheerful, which was a relief to me since I hated seeing her cry weeks ago. She's practically a new person. I guessed Noah has a good impact on her. She asked me if I was going to the hair show from the Curly Hair Club. She received an invite to the show by Stacy and thought she should ask me to tag along.

"You know I am." I laughed.

"That's awesome because we can go together with our boyfriends."

"That sounds like a good plan."

The hair show was fairytale themed which I thought was very cool. It was also next weekend. I didn't expect it to approach that fast. I thought I might have something to wear but like always I wanted to shop. With limited time I thought I would look in my closet and see what was there. I had to ask babe if he was going as well, couldn't go dateless. I knew he'd enjoy it; let's hope he wanted to go. I texted Jeremy and asked him. He immediately said he would love to join which made my heart delighted. He asked me how I was adjusting to my new life, and I responded with fine. I thanked him for the food and told him he was a chef.

"No problem, it was my pleasure."

I'm actually adjusting well. This was a new normal for me. Everything I thought I knew about myself had now altered. Something in me changed and the Afua I thought I knew was no more. My only fear was that people would view me as mentally ill and treat me differently as a result. When I thought about it, that showed how ignorant the person must be to think that way. People with mental illnesses deserved to be treated with respect just as anyone else. I was lost in thought when I received a text message from Josephine and Charlotte. They both texted and said how worried they were about me. They said they hadn't heard from me in a while and figured something was wrong. I was surprised, thinking maybe they knew what happened to me.

"Sorry to make you both worry about me. I have been going through a lot for the past few weeks."

They were both concerned about me and wanted to know what was going on. I told them how I had a mental breakdown and ended up in the hospital for two weeks.

They were shocked and told me they couldn't believe that happened to me. They insisted on doing a FaceTime call with me. I didn't want to because I felt embarrassed, but caved in. Josephine started off with a prayer and the rest of us followed. We were intensively praying about a lot of things, such as my situation, school, career, etc. I felt good casting all my worries to God. I was crying and asking God to change my situation and use me as a vessel to inspire people one day. I wanted to empower people with mental illnesses to always strive for the best and not look down on themselves. After we finished praying, we updated one another on what was going on in each other's lives. It felt so good talking with them and laughing about old times in the church. We talked about the little crush I used to have on Donald. I thought he had a crush on me too because of how he would treat me, but he was just being nice. We had a nickname for him, which we kept a secret for a long time and still do. I couldn't say his nickname for fear that people would start calling him this name. These were my girls for real. It was refreshing talking to them. After I got off the phone, I fell asleep.

The next morning my alarm woke me up. It was so loud that I was startled. Thank God I was the only one in the room when this happened. I decided that today I would be on go mode, meaning I was going to accomplish finishing these assignments at all costs. I quickly got myself ready and was out the door. Contrary to my normal routine of going to the library, I decided to go to one of the academic buildings I hadn't been to before. There was a lot of space and quiet enough for me to concentrate. I got a lot of work done, which surprised me. Then I realized I was hungry and went on the shuttle to get McDonald's. I got a quarter pounder with bacon and cheese, large fries and a McFlurry. I'd eat dessert anytime. I walked back to the shuttle stop and headed back to campus. On my way to the dorm, I got a call from Akosua. She was telling me how she heard I wasn't doing good from her mother, which is my other aunt, Felicia. I told my cousin that she shouldn't worry because I was doing fine after my ordeal just a few weeks ago.

She was inquiring about what happened and I told her. I knew she would gossip but I didn't care because I knew myself and was self-assured. She was sad about it and told me she would keep me in prayers. I thanked her and told her I appreciated the phone call. It meant a lot to me to have her check up on me. The rest of the day was spent doing what I do best, watching TV shows. *Living Single* was the show of choice, and I didn't regret it. Two days later, I received a call from a woman named Mrs. Morgan from the outpatient clinic at the nearby hospital. She wanted to ask me some intake questions about some of the symptoms I was experiencing beforehand. I didn't feel like answering questions, but I did anyways because I was taught to answer when an elder or professional was talking to you. This was to show respect. She gave me my appointment for next month and told me to pick up my medication at the local pharmacy. She told me the medication was supposed to help with my depression.

So, I asked Jeremy if he could take me to Rite Aid to pick up my prescription. Before I could even blink, he was at my door ready to go. We walked to his car, and he told me how he missed talking and spending time with me. He apologized to me for not being very responsive via text because he was busy with work and club responsibilities. Jeremy was always honest with me and let me know everything. I didn't mind that we hadn't spoken much in days because I was secure within myself. Plus, I loved my alone time to work, do assignments, and relax. We always enjoyed our time together and it felt like time hadn't passed at all. Once we arrived at the pharmacy, I noticed that there was a long line of people. We waited patiently, anticipating our turn. Eventually, we were next. There was a man at the counter. He wore glasses and had this piercing look in his eyes.

I could tell he wasn't in the mood, but surprisingly as soon as we made eye contact, he smiled and said, "How might I help you?"

I told him I wanted to pick up my prescription. He asked me for my name and date of birth. He also asked for my insurance card, which I handed to him. He handed me my medicine and card. He told me that the information about my medicine was in the bag. I signed for my prescription, and I was out the door. Jeremy asked me if I would like to watch the movie *Till* tonight. I agreed because I had nothing planned for the rest of the day.

One of my love languages happened to be quality time. I loved spending time with my significant other even if it meant doing nothing. Every time I was with him, I felt safe and that was an amazing feeling to have with someone. We drove back to campus and Jeremy reminded me of our date plans and told me to get ready soon. I went to my room to get ready for date night. I figured that since it would be a sad movie, I shouldn't wear makeup because knowing me, I would cry it off. I opted for something casual so I could be comfy watching the movie. I heard the door opening and it was Melissa. She was smiling from ear to ear, so I knew she was in the best mood. She said hello and asked me where I was going. I told her I was watching the movie *Till* with Jeremy.

She was all smiles being that I was going out, since I'd been working on assignments for days. I thought of how far Melissa and I have come, because before, our relationship sucked. Never would've thought in a million years we'd be on good terms. Now she'd made a whole 180 and changed her attitude ever since she met Noah. I tell you, that man rubbed off on her in a positive way. Anyways, I headed to Jeremy's room and knocked on it. His roommate answered and let me in. The room was nice and neat. It smelled really good too, which was a shock since I assumed guys were messy.

The colors of the room were mainly green and blue. Jeremy was ready and told me he just needed to grab his keys. We walked out the room and down the stairs. As we walked to the car, I just couldn't stop thinking about how lucky I was to have an amazing man in my life. After all I'd been through, he was still here and for that I would forever respect him. We got in the car and proceeded to the Regal movie theater. The drive there wasn't bad at all. Jeremy opened the doors for me, which was chivalrous of him. He paid for the whole date and didn't let me pay at all. That's typical of him; even when I offered at times, he declined my plea. Jeremy had already paid for the tickets in advance online. All we had to do was show them and pay for our snacks. Jeremy and I both got popcorn and a slushie. We walked to our designated theater and found our seats.

The movie previews were showing which was good cause it meant we came just in time. All I could say: when the movie got to the sad parts, it made me cry. I mean it was sad when a mother found out her own child died due to racism. The woman who claimed he catcalled or flirted with her lied. I wished justice was served for his family because it wasn't fair. It hit me hard, and I couldn't explain my feelings I began weeping. I was an empath, so I felt things extra hard when someone was feeling sad. Jeremy tried to console me, and it worked for a while. After the movie, we decided to get food to eat because we were kind of hungry since we barely touched our food.

Jeremy suggested we go to Dave & Busters to enjoy ourselves. We needed that after watching such a sad but powerful movie. We arrived at the place and are greeted by a man, who was very nice and told us we were a beautiful couple. I was flattered and smiled so hard. He seated us at our table and gave us the menu. He asked us what we liked to drink, and I immediately said cranberry juice while Jeremy decided he would get lemonade. The waiter left to get us our drinks as I proceeded to look at the menu and make my choice. I usually opted for a burger, but today I felt a bit spontaneous. I wanted to try something new. That's when I spotted voodoo pasta and I was like, "Definitely trying this!"

Jeremy, on the other hand, chose parmesan chicken. Moments later, the waiter came with our drinks, and we told him what we each wanted. The waiter told me that the voodoo pasta was amazing which reassured me I made the right choice. I was very picky when it came to food. Trying this was a big deal.

Jeremy and I talked about the upcoming event happening on

campus from the Curly Hair Club. It's called "Happily Ever After" since it's a princess/fairytale themed show. We both didn't know what we would wear. So, we decided to go to the mall tomorrow to look for something. I usually planned ahead for events like this, but my life had been hectic. Finally, our food came, and it looked delicious. I tried my pasta, and it tasted good. The flavor in my mouth is something I couldn't explain. Jeremy liked his food but wanted to try mine, and I let him. He enjoyed mine more than his own food, which was funny to me. Eventually, he finished his food. He paid for the food and we were out the door.

We headed back to campus and along the way we jammed to music. I always enjoyed times like this. It made me happy being around this man. Love could make you feel a kind of way that you couldn't explain. Today was a great day for me. Once we arrived on campus, we sat in the car for a little while before getting out. He got out and opened my door, gave me a kiss, and we walked towards the dorm. He also gave me a hug and told me he'd see me in the morning. I walked down to my room and opened the door and found that Melissa wasn't there. So, I used the opportunity to just relax and watch *New Amsterdam.* As I watched my show, I heard the door knock and when I checked the peephole, it was Stacy. I let her in. She was checking up on me to see how I was doing. I appreciated it because this showed she cared.

Stacy asked me how I was adjusting to the schoolwork since I came back, and I told her honestly, it was a little overwhelming, all the work I had to do, but I knew I could do it.

"Afua, I know you can do all things through Christ that strengthens you. Never forget that."

Then she left. I spend the rest of the night planning how I'd finish all my schoolwork before break. I woke up the next morning feeling exhausted but all that didn't matter to me since I would be with my love soon. He texted me good morning and asked if I'd be ready soon. I quickly took a shower and got ready. I threw anything on at this point, because ya girl is going shopping. I texted Jeremy and told him I was ready. He told me to meet him at the main lobby. We met up and headed to the car like usual.

Did I say it yet? We were headed to the Cross Gates Mall. I'd been there before, but never to shop, so this shall be exciting. Jeremy found a parking spot and we walked into the mall. It was fairly early so not too many people were there. Once we got inside, I was like a kid in a candy store. I wanted to see all the stores. The first place we entered was Forever 21. I had a few choices to wear. I thought I'd find something there. Everything looked nice, but I didn't find anything that fit my aesthetic. So, we moved on to the next store, Macy's, and all we could find was formal stuff which were kind of expensive, and some outfits were just not my style. Jeremy also found the same issue. I nearly gave up until I saw Zara. I went inside and was like, *This is my style.* I spotted an asymmetrical dress that had orange, white, and black colors on it. I took it and went to the dressing room. I tried it on, and it fit like a glove, plus the orange against my melanin made me look like a fine babe.

Then it was time to get Jeremy something to match. I got outside and found Jeremy an orange animal print shirt and khaki pants that looked nice. He tried it on and told me he liked the outfit. I realized I had shoes to match and so did Jeremy. We bought our items and went to the food court. Jeremy wanted to try Charley's and I was down for it. I ordered a steak Philly cheesesteak and a peach lemonade, while Jeremy got a bacon 3 cheesesteak and a strawberry lemonade. We found a table and sat down to eat. Honestly, I was skeptical about the food because I'd never had a cheesesteak, but to my surprise, it was good. Jeremy liked his as well, but I preferred the strawberry lemonade a bit more than the peach. After eating, we walked back to the car and blasted some music as usual. I'd been playing the song "Sugarcane" by Camidoh on repeat and it was a bop, especially the remix.

We arrived on campus, but like always, I didn't want to leave. So, we just sat in the car for a little bit, talking about Thanksgiving break. Jeremy said he'd drive me down to Brooklyn. It would be our first road trip together. We also decided we would go to the African student organization's pageant/fashion show in the upcoming weeks. I was so excited that I started grinning. We got out of the car and headed to the dorms. I was just thinking about how cute I'd look for the Curly Hair Club show. Jeremy gave me a hug and a kiss and left. I loved it when he hugged me. It always smelled amazing in his arms; I felt like time stood still. That was my man for sure, I told myself. The rest of the day was spent working on my assignments. I was almost done with them. I just needed to work on the rest tomorrow.

I realized I hadn't seen Melissa much in the past day or two. I figured she was hanging out with Noah or at hockey practice. Just when I was getting ready for bed, I heard the fire alarm go off. I knew what that meant. We had to go outside until a professional turned off the alarm and gave us clearance to go back inside. As a result of the loud fire alarm going off, I got so angry that my face felt hot, and my head hurt at the alarm's screeching noise. So, I quickly gathered myself and left the dorm along with the rest of the students. As we waited outside, I spotted Jeremy and his roommate. I walked over and greeted them. Jeremy asked me if I was okay, and I told him my head hurt and I was tired. He wanted to help me but couldn't. He suggested I sleep it off when we got back inside. According to him, someone in our dorm was making popcorn and wasn't paying attention to it, which triggered the fire alarm. I shook my head because I couldn't understand how someone could be irresponsible like that. He said it happened a lot last year because people didn't pay attention to what they were doing.

We stood outside for twenty minutes before we were told we could go inside. I quickly bolted to my room and fell asleep. The following week was a blur to me. I finished my assignments and sent them to my professors. Then I went to work and class—it was a fast-paced week. The only thing I was happy about was the hair show.

The day of the show was really hectic. Melissa and I got ready together. I put on my eye contacts because I wanted a different look. I did my makeup and put on my clothes carefully, so as to not ruin my makeup. I searched through my shoes and found a nice heel that was comfortable to wear. It was an orange heel that had straps. It matched the outfit perfectly. My hair was in braids, so I just did a side part. Melissa was wearing a light blue dress and her makeup looked immaculate. We took pictures of one another. I really liked the pictures Melissa took of me.

"You're my photographer," I told her, and she just laughed.

I sprayed on my Burberry Her perfume, which is one of my faves. I texted Jeremy to see if he was ready. He was just waiting for me.

I asked Melissa when Noah was meeting us, and she said, "He'll meet us at the event. He's running late."

We met up with Jeremy and walked over to the college center. There was a line forming to get inside, which amazed me. I assumed we would be the first ones here. We waited in line and eventually it was our turn to show our online tickets. The girl taking the tickets looked at Jeremy, then at me, and rolled her eyes. After that she proceeded to laugh. She said something to the girl sitting next to her. They both looked us up and down.

I looked over at Jeremy and he said, "Just ignore her."

"Ignore her? She was being rude and petty."

Melissa said, "Afua, did you just see the look that girl gave you? She must be pressed about something." When we got inside, Jeremy told me that was his ex and she wasn't over the breakup, even though it was a year ago.

I wanted to ask him more questions, but I would rather not let this person ruin my time at this event. He told me about her, but I didn't know she would act like this towards us.

She was a nobody, if I'm being honest. *To still be harboring bad feelings towards your ex was crazy, but that wasn't my problem,* I thought. The decorations were wonderfully done. There were flowers everywhere and a backdrop to take pictures that said *happily ever after* with a castle and sparkles. The stage was decorated as well. We found seats in the second row near the stage, which was good for us. A few moments later Noah came in and he was dressed nice with this hint of blue in his outfit. He matched with Melissa just like Jeremy and I. Melissa introduced Noah to Jeremy and they got along pretty well. Half an hour later, the show began. The host of the show was a man who was tall and lighter in complexion. He had on a nice black suit. His name was Sir. He made the event lively and fun.

Every time he was on stage, he had this aura about him. Sir would make us laugh every time. Remember when I said the theme of the show was fairytale? Well, they made it come to life. Each girl that walked across the stage was a Disney princess or character. I saw Stacy and Alyssa, who looked beautiful in their hair and makeup. I was cheering for them when they got on stage. At one point they had a segment showing hairstylists styling people's hair in under twenty minutes and the audience picked whoever was the best one. The winner was a girl named Brandy and to be honest, she did an amazing job. She did a nice fishtail braid which was simple yet elegant. I forgot to mention that during the intermission, they brought out snacks and desserts. I only got a cupcake, but it was very flavorful and yummy.

After the show, we decided to take some pictures. Next thing I knew, Jeremy's ex was standing by me. I was confused because I didn't even know her. She talked to him and told him something. All I heard was Jeremy tell her that he had a girlfriend, and he wasn't interested. I was very elated that my man defended me. I was about to look at him sideways if he didn't. Jeremy walked over to me and told me that his ex was being weird, asking him if he would want to get back together with her. He declined her advances and now she was salty about it. We continued taking our pictures and I got a picture with my man. While I did so, I saw girls looking at me, but I ignored them because they weren't going to bring me down. We decided to go to the after party off campus. This would be my second party ever in college. Noah drove us to the party, and we enjoyed ourselves. I stayed glued to Jeremy the whole night, dancing with him. They played "I'm Still In Love With You" by Sean Paul and I began singing to Jeremy. We enjoyed the vibes at this party. They were playing oldies and newer music. The night was very much a blur, but it was fun.

Nine

Promise Ring

"Hey girl, I haven't seen you in forever! Can I get a hug?"

I turned around and saw McKenzie. "Girl, I missed you so much!"

She asked, "How have you been? Did you get caught up on assignments?"

"I did. I'm just taking life one day at a time. It's been really challenging," I told her.

"Why do you say that?" she asked. I whispered to her that I'd been diagnosed with bipolar disorder and depression.

McKenzie, not knowing how to react, just said, "I'm very sorry you went through that. Is that why I haven't seen much of you lately?"

"Yes," I said.

"We should really hang out sometime, if you want," she said.

I agreed since it's been a while. I figured it would get my mind off things. She asked me what I was doing for Thanksgiving break. I would be hanging out with my family and friends.

McKenzie asked if we could hang out in the city, and I said, "Of course!"

We had to plan what we were doing though since there was so much to do in the city. I asked her where she lived, and she said Harlem. We could always do something fun in Manhattan or any borough. We'd iron out the details later. I was in the library working when I saw Alyssa and Stacy. They saw me and walked over, and we talked about the show. I told them how amazing they did, and they began to smile.

Stacy said that hours of practice made it all happen.

She asked me if I went to the after party and I said, "You bet I did!"

They began laughing at me. Alyssa said, "Not to gossip or anything, but do you know Jeremy's ex Juliet was there? And she told us how you two were dancing with each other."

"I had no idea she was at the party. However, I met her for the first time, and she wasn't so kind. If you catch my drift."

"I know, which is why I asked Juliet why she's so jealous about her ex moving on. She said he was her first everything and when they broke up due to her insecurities, she was devastated." I felt bad but I realized she had a problem with me and even tried to ask my boyfriend to get back with her.

Honestly, I couldn't care less, but I didn't tell Stacy and Alyssa that. I just said, "Oh, I see."

We talked for a few minutes until they left. During my shift, I worked on some assignments and helped a few people with research. The next day was the appointment I dreaded having with Mrs. Morgan at the mental health outpatient clinic. When I walked in, I went to the main desk where the secretary was and gave her my name. I told her I was seeing Mrs. Morgan. I waited for a total of twenty-five minutes before I was seen.

This reminded me of when I used to go to therapy. How eager I was to actually attend, but here I was feeling all these emotions. I was still reluctant to go back, being that I had a bad experience with Dr. Stevens. Well, she did save my life, but the whole ordeal made me appear crazy. I was embarrassed that I reacted that way to being helped. Being in denial was the worst thing I could've done in that situation. We all knew I wasn't in the right state of mind, but I suppressed it for so long until I cracked. My anxiety kicked in and my heart was beating fast. Surely Mrs. Morgan might have her preconceived judgements towards me. I mean, she had my chart and knew what happened to me. Let me distract myself while I waited for my named to be mentioned.

I was on my phone when I heard my name being called. I looked up and it's a brown-skinned black woman with curly shoulder length hair and hazel eyes.

She smiled at me and said, "Afua, I'm ready for you."

I followed Mrs. Morgan to her office and sat on the chair. She introduced herself to me and said she would be the one seeing me from now on at the outpatient clinic. She asked me how the medicine was working for me. I told her I was only aware of the medicine I picked up at the pharmacy, which was for my depression. She told me that the injection I would receive today was for my bipolar disorder. She also asked if I experienced any side effects such as experiencing delusions, suicidal thoughts, etc.

I said, "No not to my knowledge."

She asked me what I do for fun. I usually watched TV shows or go on dates with my boyfriend. Her face lit up when I said I had a boyfriend. She asked, "How long have you both been dating for?"

I said one going on two months. I thought she was being inquisitive at this point, because she asked if he knows about my diagnosis, and I said, "Yes, he's been by my side the whole time."

She told me that it was amazing I had support. Her follow up question was, "How do you feel about having bipolar disorder and depression?"

I was honest with her when I said, "I feel like this is a burden on my life. I will have this forever, and it won't go away."

She looked at me and said, "Well Afua, you are more than capable of living a great fulfilling life. Do you believe in God?" I said yes. "Always remember that God gives us what we can handle. Maybe this is a testimony to help others going through the same thing. All you have to do is keep up with your appointments and take care of yourself."

During this time, I felt seen and heard. I mean, everyone in my life was helpful, which I would forever be grateful. Mrs. Morgan walked me to the nurse's office. I later found out that her name was Mrs. Graham but she went by nurse Graham. She was very kind. She looked excited to see me. She tried to get to know me in the span of a few minutes. After that, she asked me which arm I want my shot. I said the left and she prepared the medicine and used an alcohol wipe on the area. She asked me if I was ready for my shot before injecting me. I could feel the medicine go in my arm. It didn't hurt until I got to my dorm room. I felt a bit tired, so I slept the entire day.

When I woke up it was nighttime. I got a call from Jeremy, and he asked if I was alright. I told him I fell asleep after my appointment. I saw that he texted me five times. Jeremy was really worried about me.

He asked how it went, and I said, "Fine, the ladies I met were very nice and I look forward to seeing them next month."

"That fashion show with the African Student Organization—are we still going?" he asked.

I immediately said yes.

He asked which outfit we were wearing.

"It's a good thing you asked. I already reached out to my seamstress via WhatsApp and she's already sewing the dress for me. It's an off the shoulder dress that is all red and beaded."

Jeremy wanted to know if I could get his measurements and send it to the seamstress to make him an outfit. I texted Maame Yaa and she said she'd be happy to make his outfit. I really was excited to showcase my outfit. I mean, go big or go home, that was my motto. I wanted to showcase kente (Ghanaian cloth) to the world.

I was thrilled the next day for sign language class. We learned how to develop elaborate sentences. I partnered up with a girl named Lola and we practiced doing various sentences. We were told that for our final exam, we'd have to tell a story in sign. I knew that I would have to practice for weeks to perfect my story. I wondered what story I could tell. After class I felt exhausted, so I went to sleep shortly after. It was the best nap I'd had in a while. I felt energized and ready to work on my assignments. I worked on them until I got tired again. I was the most productive I'd been all semester. I decided to reward myself by watching my favorite show until I fell asleep.

A few days later, Jeremy decided to take me to the New York State Museum. It was good, looking at the exhibitions and learning more about history, including different figures such as Berenice Abbott. Her series called "Changing New York" was really nice, seeing how New York used to look in the 1900s. Especially looking at the other exhibition called "Black Capital: Harlem in the 1920s" was very intriguing. After our time in the museum, we went to get some food at Five Guys. We decided to sit in the restaurant and just talk. I got the grilled cheeseburger with bacon, which has been trending on TikTok. Jeremy, being a copycat, wanted the same thing.

Then he said, "Babe, you know I been wanting to try it."

"Whatever." I rolled my eyes and we both started to laugh. We also got Oreo cookies and a salted caramel milkshake with fries. Let me tell you, when I say that grilled cheeseburger was good, it truly was. In fact, both of us enjoyed our meal. We talked about our relationship and how we could make it better for the two of us.

Our relationship wasn't perfect, but we tried to be more understanding of one another. If we had a disagreement, which wasn't often, we talked about it and saw where the issue lies. We understood each other, I guess you could say we were two peas in a pod. That's my right hand. This was my first relationship and so far, it was going well. I never thought I'd be in a relationship so soon, but things happen in mysterious ways. I was learning a lot about myself and how to love someone. He taught me how to love parts about myself I didn't think I could. We finished eating and were on our way back to campus. As always, I dreaded going back because I didn't want the day to end with him. Just as I was thinking the day was over, he suggested we watch a TV show or movie together in his room. I was down for it since I looked forward to our dates. We walked to his room, and it was clean and tidy like the last time I was there. There was a smart TV in the middle of the window on top of one of the dressers. Jeremy handed me the remote and I proceeded to check through the apps and settled on Netflix. We watched a crime documentary about a son who killed his father. It came out that the father was maltreating him. The father never enrolled him in traditional learning, so there was a lot he didn't know how to do until his stepmother came into the picture. It was a very interesting but sad documentary. We were going to watch the Jeffrey Dahmer docuseries, but I decided against it because it was too gruesome, the details of his crimes. Can you believe he ate people? Anyways, we decided to watch *Manifest,* which was nice. We cuddled together and then things got hot and heavy. I'm not going to say too much, but we were making out until I stopped him 'cause we're both on a celibacy journey.

He was apologetic but I didn't mind. I just brushed the situation off because it wasn't intentional. I'm not a saint; deep down inside, I knew I wanted things to go further, but I had to keep to our goal of no sex before marriage. When I tell you that was difficult, it really was, especially when you had attraction to someone so bad the feelings took over you. Lucky for us, his roommate wasn't in the room, so there was no awkwardness. Eventually it became night, and I was growing tired and me hene (a nickname I started calling him recently; it means my king in Twi) even noticed. I hadn't called him Teddy in a while. I figured this other name suited him well. Jeremy called me his Queen in return. He decided to walk me down to my room and I knocked out shortly after. I woke up feeling well rested.

A few minutes passed and I got a call from my mom. She said, "Afua, so if I don't call you, you wouldn't think to call me?"

I apologized and realized my fault because I'd been so occupied with life I forgot to reach out to my family. She inquired about my wellbeing and school. I told her how I finished all my assignments I got an extension on, and my mom said, "We thank God. That boy you're dating, Jeremy, is very respectful. Your father and I like him."

I felt awkward talking to my mom about my relationship. Even though I knew she was understanding, she might tell things to my dad, which I didn't appreciate. "Yes, Mommy. I agree he's respectful and kind. He has always treated me right since the day I met him."

"I hope that never changes. I know this is an intrusive question, but are you and Jeremy sexually active? It's okay, you can tell me."

I was completely shocked cause that was none of her business. "Mommy, we haven't done anything. You should trust me more."

"You are my daughter, and I want the best for you. So if there's something you need to tell me, feel free."

I got her concern about my wellbeing but she was being a bit too intrusive into my dating life. My mom and I talked for a few minutes more. "Afua, you know it's important to pray daily. Never forget your prayers."

"Yes, Mommy, I know."

"Let me pray for you then. I pray that God has his hands over every part of your life. May you lack nothing in life. Everything you are working towards is for a purpose and may it be fulfilled. In Jesus' name we pray, amen. Let God be with you."

I loved it when my mom prayed for me. I would forever be grateful for her despite the fact we bumped heads sometimes. After our conversation, I went to work. It wasn't a bad shift. I got to work with McKenzie, and it was a blast.

"You know, I couldn't go to the Curly Hair Club show because of a family emergency."

I was concerned for her. "Is everything alright with you and your family?"

"My brother had a health scare which shocked the family." She didn't want to go into detail, and I wasn't going to push further.

I could see tears form in her eyes and I didn't want to further make her reminisce on the recent events in her life. "I will keep your family in my prayers."

"Thank you. I will make sure to be at the African student organization pageant."

"That's good, because so will I."

"We should go together." I agreed because McKenzie is fun. She was a vibe all by herself. We started talking about Thanksgiving break. "There's this one place I've been meaning to go to called Black Tap, which is a burger and milkshake restaurant."

"I haven't been there before."

"Neither have I, but I heard it was good."

"I think we'll have a nice time hanging out."

Work went by fast; before I knew it, my shift was over. McKenzie and I walked out together, said bye to one another, and then went our separate ways.

I went back to my room, and I saw that Melissa was there. She told me about her date with Noah and how their relationship was going well. I was happy for her, but I still felt that she didn't get enough time to heal from her last break up.

I guessed everyone was different and healed at their own pace. Some people didn't know how to be single because they feared being alone. I just wished her the best instead of being a downer about the situation. I just told her that was amazing. She also told me how she'd never felt this way about any guy she dated. She said her last boyfriend Todd made her realize she needed to focus on building her self-worth and esteem. It was because of him she didn't trust Noah right away. According to her, he gained her trust by being honest about everything. He told her about past relationships and expressed his intentions of wanting to be exclusive at some point. I think it was amazing how people were placed just at the right time for you to meet them. Then I thought about Jeremy and how it was a weird coincidence that we even met.

We legit bumped into one another, became friends, and then boom—a relationship. It all happened fast. Melissa seemed very happy telling me her business. I respected that, but I couldn't see us being good friends if her attitude didn't change. In Ghana, they have a saying about a person's character. In Twi, the saying is, "suban te sɛ nyinsɛn a wuntumi mfansie." That meant character was like pregnancy: you cannot hide it. If you had bad character, there was nothing that could conceal it. I laid in my bed and watched a movie on my iPad, which happened to be *Matilda*. I liked the part when Matilda got adopted by the teacher, Miss Honey. I always thought it was messed up how Matilda's parents treated her. Her father was a crook, and her mother was oblivious to Matilda's needs. Can we talk about how wicked the principal Ms. Trunchbull was? I was surprised none of the parents knew what was going on. Days passed by and all I did was go to class and work.

It wasn't long before it was Thanksgiving break. I wasn't playing about packing my clothes for the week. I was ready before Jeremy even called me to meet him in the main lobby. Like the gentleman he was, Jeremy took my luggage and put it in the trunk. We went to McDonald's to get breakfast. I got a steak, egg, and cheese sandwich on a bagel with hash browns and orange juice. Jeremy got the same thing, but only got a sausage egg and cheese McGriddle. We were a couple that loved food. I was surprised I hadn't gained relationship weight. After that, we were headed to the gas station. Me being who I was, I had to go into the store and get some snacks for the road. I got Sour Patch Kids, Doritos, salt and pepper chips, orange Fanta, Coke, and Reese's. Jeremy and I would share the snacks. Once Jeremy was done putting gas in the tank, we were on the road, headed to NYC. I played music using the playlist with songs we usually listened to. The first song to play was "Overdose" by Mavins. We were both singing and enjoying ourselves. An hour into our drive, and I was feeling good. We had some good conversations about life and what we envision our future being like. I just wanted to be successful in what I did and help people who were struggling with mental health. Jeremy said that my dream would come true. I just had to believe that I would attract those things in my life. He believed in me and because of that, I felt like I could do anything. The next hour, I was growing tired, so I took a nap. I didn't realize I fell asleep until it was the final hour, and we were close to the city. I was so anxious to see my family. Finally, we were almost at my house. I live near Kings Highway in Brooklyn. It was a five-bedroom home. We moved there about two years ago. Before that we were in a two-bedroom apartment.

I remembered those moments there; we really struggled. Life only started to get better for us when my dad got a new job, and my mom finished nursing school. This was a major blessing to our family. We finally arrived at my house. Jeremy got my luggage and brought them upstairs. He greeted my mom, who was home. She couldn't contain her smile! She was so happy to see him. My siblings were at school and didn't get to meet him. I told Jeremy to call me when he got home so I knew he was safe. Driving wasn't easy and it could be dangerous driving in NYC because there were so many reckless drivers. Once he left, it was just me and my mom. She gave me a hug and told me how much she missed me. She told me that everyone was excited to see me and had been anticipating my arrival for days. Hearing that warmed my heart and made me realize how fortunate I was. My family was proud of me and wanted to see me succeed.

I headed to my room and just relaxed for the meantime. My room was just as I left it, so I decided to tidy up the room. I remembered when I was leaving for school, I was in a rush and didn't think about the state of my room. I put on some '90s music and look what comes on: "Cupid" by 112. I loved the beginning; it reminded me of a spoken word I wrote. I titled it "Love" and it went like this:

Love was the only thing that mattered. That four-letter word so sweet there's a day for it. Some might say that's for lovers. At any given moment, you can bestow love to the people who matter. L.O.V.E., you cross my mind a million times. Yet the very time I'm supposed to practice self-love, you vanish away. Without a trace, I'm left stranded. "Love yourself first," they say; such a simple phrase that holds meaning. How do you love yourself when the world has made you hate the very skin you're in? Told you're not pretty, smart, or talented enough. The words meant to encourage now a distant memory. I miss the warm embrace of those words that sent my spirit soaring. I lost the element of who I am. Like, who is she? I want her back. Searching for what was lost, yet welcoming what's yet to come. This spoken word had me thinking about writing more. I thought I could actually publish my work or speak for a crowd, but it was just a thought.

That song simply had an effect on my feelings and made me reflect on my diagnosis and how Jeremy hadn't left me. I heard from other people that normally relationships didn't work when they heard news like this. I guessed this young man really loved me. I couldn't seem to shake the feeling that I was a burden to him, but he hadn't complained yet. I was jamming to my music when I got a knock on the door.

I lowered my music and said, "Come in."

My mom was standing there and asked if she could talk to me. "I know the recent change of things in your life, with your diagnosis and all. I love you, Afua, but can I be honest? I am worried about you."

"I promise I'm taking care of myself. Recently I went to the outpatient clinic to start my treatment. So, I have been taking responsibility of myself. No need to worry."

"How was it?"

"The people that work there are nice and give good advice. I feel seen and heard. I have also been taking my pills every day."

"How do you feel about your diagnosis?"

"I feel like this is a curse, which gets me down at times."

"My dear, never feel like having bipolar disorder and depression is a curse. Things happen out of our control, but who knows? You can help others by telling your story. That is why it's important that you don't give up."

My mom wasn't the first person to say that. It had me thinking of the best way to tell my story. "Do you still want to stay upstate for college? Wouldn't it be nice to transfer to a local college in NYC next semester? You will be surrounded by family and friends here, and you can transfer your medical treatment to a nearby hospital."

"Mommy, my position still stands on the matter. I want to stay at college."

My mom saw that she couldn't change my mind, so she switched the topic. "What will you be cooking for Thanksgiving?"

"I'll probably end up making mac and cheese and chicken." I actually didn't mind cooking. If it wasn't for my dorm having one kitchen, I'd be cooking on the daily.

"I would like for you, Penelope, and possibly Chloe to help me prep the food." She was making meat pie, bofrot (Ghanaian donut), and jollof rice with goat meat. She might make more if she was up for it. My mom exited my room, leaving me to go back to my music and cleaning. I actually ended up cleaning my whole room and placing my suitcase in my closet. Suddenly, I got a text from Jeremy telling me he reached home safely.

He asked if we could go out one of these days if I wasn't too busy. I was so ecstatic, I let out a scream and said, "Of course!" I wondered where we could go in the city. There was a lot to do. I knew he would plan something fun for us. I got another knock on my door and it was my siblings. They were home from school. Each of them gave me a hug.

"We missed you so much," Penelope said. Chloe and Kwabena both agree.

"I missed you all too." My siblings and I loved one another and were big on togetherness. We'd always been a tight-knit family, since we're basically all we got. Especially since most of our family either lived in different cities or in Ghana.

"So how was the drive down here?" Kwabena asked.

"It was tiring, but not bad. I was the passenger queen."

They chuckled a little. "When are you gonna get your driver's license?"

"I have other priorities right now, so maybe winter break or in the summer, I'll learn."

Penelope rolled her eyes and said, "Girl, you know you'll never learn."

"I bet I can prove you wrong!" They left my room after that.

I spent my time relaxing and watching a sermon by Sarah Jakes Roberts. She spoke to my soul. She said the only way I could become was to undo. That meant undoing things that stifled growth, such as low self-esteem, fear of inadequacy, and abandonment. I listened to worship music; one of my favorites was Diana Hamilton. In her song "Work In Progress," she really was inspiring. I reflected on those words. I then picked up my Bible and began to read, and stumbled across Mathew 21:22, which read, "Whatever you ask for in prayer, you will receive, if you have faith." It reminded me that even when things seemed bleak, I had to keep believing that things would change. The fact that I was alive after that traumatic experience was a blessing. Many people didn't get the help that they needed and suffered in silence, but I was fortunate to have someone help me. I got a knock on my door from Chloe telling me that dinner was ready.

We would be eating light soup with fufu and assorted meat. She didn't have to tell me twice, I ran downstairs and grabbed my bowl. I began pouring the soup and meat into my bowl. I could hear Kwabena telling me to make sure I didn't take all the meat. I told him I would save him the tiniest pieces and began laughing.

He was like, "Man whatever, all I know is you better leave some for the rest of us."

I took my food and sat at the island in our kitchen. I enjoyed my food. The flavors captivated my mouth. It was a little spicy, but nothing I couldn't handle. I finished my food and felt satisfied. Then I washed my dishes and stayed in the living room. My siblings and I wanted to watch a movie together. I grabbed the remote and browsed through Netflix's movie section. Every movie I suggested, someone didn't like it.

Finally, we agree on watching *The Nutty Professor*. It was a movie about an overweight professor who created a formula that altered his appearance, but more things happened. His personality also changed because he was a different person known as Buddy. It was a very funny movie. I'd only seen it once, but I remembered enjoying it. The movie started and everyone was hooked. Even my mom liked some aspects of the movie. I heard the door open and it was my dad. I ran to give him a hug. He asked me when I came home, and I told him a few hours ago. He had a big smile on his face and said he missed me. He said he was tired from work and wanted to get some food. He noticed we were watching a movie and wanted me to get back to watching it.

It was a great night being home. We all had banter and shared laughs about past experiences we encountered together. I remembered when I was younger, my dad took us to a nearby park where we used to live. We saw an ice cream truck and asked if we could have some. He got us each a scoop of ice cream, but Chloe's scoop fell. When I tell you this girl cried bloody murder and then had the nerve to try and steal Penelope's ice cream. We reflected on that and began to laugh. Chloe till this day was obsessed with ice cream, particularly sea salt caramel. I fell asleep after and woke up feeling a little tired. My body woke me up early. I tried going back to sleep, but it didn't work out for me. So, I decided I'd catch up on schoolwork and prepare for my sign language final. I was still unsure what story I'd tell in sign. As I was thinking, a memory came to mind. I'd talk about the first time I was a flower girl at a wedding. It was a nice experience because everyone thought I did great. I also got to dance coming into the venue and was the main attraction. People were spraying me with dollar bills, it was a great time. I took a shower and got ready for the day. I went downstairs and my mom and dad were awake making breakfast. This was a shock to me because my dad rarely cooked. I guessed he must be in a good mood today. My parents made French toast, eggs, and bacon. We also had store-bought banana nut muffins. By the time I got my food, everyone in the house was awake and eating. They left me some and I began eating. It was delicious, especially the banana nut muffins. I was in love. I thanked my parents for making us breakfast and went back to my room. I did not do much that day.

However, the next day, I went to church, and I received a text from Jeremy saying he was going to come with me. No one in my house was going because my parents were busy. I made up my mind I was going, but felt a bit awkward being alone. I was elated because I did not think he'd agree, because it wasn't his home church. He said he'd be at my house in thirty minutes. We were running a bit late despite church starting at 11 am. I went to The Church of Pentecost, and they had two services. The one in the morning was English and the later one was a bilingual Twi service. I wore a nice peach peplum dress and nude heels. My bag was a bedazzled clutch that was so beautiful. I put on my nice heavy trench coat. As I was figuring out which perfume to wear, I got a phone call from Jeremy saying he was outside. I quickly grabbed my Viva La Juicy perfume and sprayed it on. Then I ran like a maniac outside.

When I saw Jeremy, I couldn't help but get this warm feeling. He embraced me with a kiss and I was over the moon. It wasn't butter-flies I felt, it was something I couldn't explain. He was my other half, my bestie. He drove us to the church and then looked around for parking. We ended up having to walk two blocks. I opened the door and saw some eyes watching me. There were some unfamiliar people, along with people I knew. I went straight to the back row with babe and sat down. We made it just in time for the word of God. The pastor was talking about having faith during trials. When you didn't have faith, you became distant, which ruined your relationship with God. He mentioned Bible verses, but two stood out to me. The first one was, "For I know the plans I have for you, declares the Lord, plans to prosper you and not to harm you, plans to give you hope and a future." This told me even in the midst of my trials, God knew where he was going to take me.

He wouldn't put me through something I couldn't handle. The second verse I liked was, "The Lord is close to the broken hearted and saves those who are crushed in spirit." I had definitely been depressed and felt like God wasn't there for me. I drew farther away from him and that's something I regretted, but I had to realize that God forgave us on the daily. The sermon was over, and it was time for offering. I pulled out my money and stood up. A deaconess I wasn't familiar with told my row we could put our offering in the bowl. The music by the choir was really nice. They started to sing, "On the mountain, in the valley, on the land and in the sea." That's when I knew it would be lit. There were people dancing azonto in the front and people with handkerchiefs, waving them in the air.

Jeremy whispered in my ear and said, "Your church is fun and on fire for the Lord." I was even dancing and singing.

The next thing I knew, it was announcement time. Then we prayed before church was over. My friends Josephine and Charlotte spotted me. They gave me a hug and I introduced them to Jeremy. They were smiling and appeared happy to meet him. They asked him what his major was, and he said chemistry. Then Charlotte asked what his future goal was with that major, and he replied that he wanted to become a chemist. They were really happy for him, saying how they needed more black people in the STEM field.

Josie asked us how we met, and I said, "We met at school. I

bumped into him on my way to the dorm. We became friends and eventually, we were in a relationship."

Josie said, "Aww, how sweet is that. Love can find you in the most random places."

More people I knew came up to me and gave me hugs. I introduced them to Jeremy. Each time I did so, they would smile at the both of us and ask questions.

We eventually left and headed back to my place. Jeremy got to meet my brother and sisters. Kwabena asked if he could talk to Jeremy privately. I didn't know what was said at the time. I later found out that Kwabena asked if he treated me right and that I was an amazing girl, so I better get treated with respect and kindness. Penelope and Chloe were excited to see him and asked when he would come over to the house to hang out. He said one day, maybe soon. Before he left, he told me on Tuesday we would be going on a surprise date.

Everyone was saying "Ooh, la la!"

I wondered what it could be?! I asked if I could get a hint, and he said no. It got me thinking of all the fun things we could do. What if it was an escape room activity? He left a few minutes later. McKenzie sent me a text reminding me that we were going to Black Tap tomorrow at 1:30 pm. I almost forgot we were hanging out. This showed my mind has been elsewhere lately. I spent the rest of the day talking and playing oware with my siblings. It was a game that is played in Ghana and parts of Africa. It was one of our favorite pastimes. I woke up the next morning feeling well rested. I had enough time to get dressed and go to the train station. All I had to do was take the Q train. McKenzie and I met up at Canal Street and walked over to Black Tap. We were greeted by a woman who sat us at our table. She gave us the menu, which we looked at for a moment before choosing our food. I got the Texan burger which has prime burger meat, bacon, aged cheddar, crispy onion rings, Sweet Baby Ray's BBQ and mayo. I also asked for a cookies' n cream supreme shake.

McKenzie got the wagyu steakhouse burger which has wagyu beef, pepper jack cheese, bacon, crispy onions, A1 sauce, and roasted garlic mayo. She got the cake shake which had a limited quantity. She was lucky we came in time to get one. We talked about how the break was going for us. She told me about Ezra and how they went out together to the Inter_IAM museum. It was an interactive art gallery that had lots of fun things to see. The only downside was, it's expensive for college students. Then they went to get some Italian food at Max's Restaurant. I told her that tomorrow I would be going on a surprise date somewhere.

She said, "Wow! That seems like fun."

The whole time, I was wondering what it could be. I knew it would be special because that was just his nature to plan things he knew I'd like. It was a great time with McKenzie.

We shared some laughs and had an intriguing conversation about traveling to different countries. We each had a list of countries we would love to travel to in the future. I came to the realization that in order for my dreams to come true, I had to work for it. The lifestyle I craved was within my reach, but first I had to study hard in school and get those degrees. McKenzie and I walked to the train station, hugged one another, then went our separate ways. It was a boring train ride. However, the next day I was anxious about the date, so I didn't sleep well. I kept thinking what the surprise could be. I got a "good morning, gorgeous" text from none other than Jeremy. He was talking about how he was excited for the date later today. He inquired about my wellbeing and I told him I was fine because if not he'd start to worry.

Jeremy told me to be ready by 4 pm. That gave me enough time to shower and get ready. I did what I felt was best which was going back to sleep for another hour or two. I mean it was only 8 am. I wake up after my nap and it was 10 am. I got ready for the day and made some breakfast for me since my siblings and parents weren't around. I made chocolate chip pancakes and eggs with cheddar cheese. It was really good. I outdid myself. I spent the rest of the time reading the book *You are a Badass* by Jen Sincero. I bought a copy after I was in the hospital, but didn't have time to finish it yet. It was a good time. Before I knew it, it was 3:50 pm. I had six missed calls from Jeremy. I didn't notice because I had my phone on silent and forgot to turn it off. I called him back and he said he was five minutes from my place. I quickly put on my clothes and ran down the stairs.

By the time I went downstairs, his car was pulling up. I ran to him and gave him the biggest hug.

He said, "Queen, why did you embrace me like this?"

"Because I care so much about you," I said.

He was all sentimental, saying how amazing it was to have a loving girlfriend like me. What Jeremy said made me smile to the point my face started to hurt. He drove us to this location that was unfamiliar to me. It was an apartment building in a nice neighborhood. Jeremy parked the car, and we rang the bell. That's when he told me we were doing a cooking class. I was beyond ecstatic. He knew me so well. Once we got buzzed in, we headed to the elevator and walked towards the apartment. We got off on the fourth floor and walked to apartment 4A. We rang the doorbell and was greeted by a lady who introduced herself as Delilah. She was a dark-skinned woman with a short blonde pixie-cut hairstyle. She was an average height. We followed behind her and walked to the kitchen, where she asked us to wash our hands.

Once we were finished, she told us what we'd be making for today. We were learning how to bake pies. There were three different kinds we'd be learning how to make: apple crumb, pecan, and chocolate s'more pie. I was really showing my baking skills. After we finished making the pies, we sat down and ate our creation.

"Are you two a couple? And if so, what's your backstory?"

My guess was that she asked out of curiosity. I said, "Yes, we are a couple. We met after I bumped into him on my way to our dorm. We shared a brief conversation which led to our friendship and then later a relationship. Jeremy has been by my side through a tough time. He showed me to love the parts of myself I couldn't." I could feel Jeremy holding my hand as I said this.

"That's a lovely way to meet. Jeremy, take care of her, she's special. Afua, from what you're saying, he's a great guy. Treat him with care as well. If you want longevity as a couple, you need to treat each other with kindness and tune out the noise of other people."

"Thank you, we really appreciate the advice." It was a great experience making pies. Jeremy and I said goodbye and then walked back to his car. On the way, Jeremy was quiet, which wasn't like him. I was wondering what happened, so I inquired, but he said he was fine. When we got to the car, I saw Jeremy go to the trunk and pull out two boxes, one small and one big. I just stared at him with a look of confusion.

In return, he just started smiling and said, "My queen, I got you these roses."

I opened the box and there were, in fact, sixteen pink roses. He told me that they last for up to a year or more.

"I love you so much and that I never imagined feeling this way about any girl."

"Aww, I feel the same way." What he did next made me shed so many tears. Jeremy gave me a promise ring. All I could think about was that promise ring song by Tiffany Evans. "Afua, I don't regret the day we met. It was by chance we met because I wasn't going to leave my room. But something told me to go outside and get some fresh air."

"That was only God, in all honesty."

"That's very true. I will never betray your trust. I always love you no matter what we go through." I was lost for words, I couldn't speak. I was stunned. All I could do was cry. Don't worry, they were happy tears. I accepted the ring. It was a heart-shaped, with diamonds around and inside.

It was beautiful and as he put the ring on my finger, the calmer I became. We kissed and embraced each other. I knew this was all happening so soon, but I believed every word he said. I hoped for longevity in this relationship, but my only worry was that people would try to separate us out of jealousy. Then my mind shifted to what Stacy and Alyssa said about Juliet. I felt like she would be a problem. Was I wrong for thinking that? I tried to get my mind off thinking about her and it kind of worked. I thought about how good Jeremy smelled.

"You're so beautiful and stunning, I wanted to tell you earlier, but I was nervous about giving you a promise ring." He got me feeling all giddy and stuff. He drove me back home, and the whole ride there I fidgeted with my ring and smiled.

When he approached my house, I got a little sad because I wanted to go somewhere with him. Jeremy kissed my hand and told me good night. I walked up the stairs and grabbed my keys out of my bag to open the door. I saw my family watching TV in the living room. My family greeted me and told me they were waiting for me to get back.

Penelope spotted the ring on my finger and asked, "What's that?"

My mom and dad, being nosey, came over and asked, "Where did you get that ring from?"

"Actually, it's a promise ring from Jeremy."

My mom said, "Well it seems like this boy is into you. I knew I liked him when we first met."

My dad said, "I can tell he really likes you, but be careful. Don't be deceived."

I knew my dad meant well and was just looking out for me. Mid-conversation, I got a text from Veronica asking if I would like to get my nails done tomorrow. I texted her, "Yes, I'm down."

I apologized to her for not reaching out sooner. My mind had been preoccupied with other things. She sent me the details of what time we were meeting and the name of the nail salon. I was so hyped to see her. We legit hadn't seen one another since before I left for college.

My brother started asking me questions. "Where did Jeremy get the money for the ring?"

I was confused and said, "I have no idea, I don't ask such questions."

He told me, "You know, you shouldn't be doing things to get stuff from your boyfriend!"

I didn't know what he was insinuating—I did, but it wasn't right. My face was hot, and my head began to hurt. I just rolled my eyes. "I don't have to do anything to be showered with love. You wouldn't know that because you don't have a girlfriend."

Everyone got quiet.

Kwabena was stunned, unable to speak. My lips started to curl up and I want to yell so bad, but my parents told us to stop arguing. They mainly scolded me because I was the oldest. I walked away and went upstairs. I laid down and thought about the fact that my father and brother weren't so supportive of my relationship. I wondered what changed with my father. He met him and I assumed he liked him, but I guessed I was wrong. I didn't know why. Jeremy was really a great guy and wouldn't dare maltreat me. My thoughts consumed me, making it almost difficult to go to sleep at first, but eventually I do. I woke up in a better mood than last night. I woke up to a missed call and text from Veronica. She said I should be ready by 12 pm. We usually met at the Avenue H station if we were going to Flatbush. The nail salon was called Majestic Queen Nails. I looked at the time and it was 10 am. I got up and took a shower. I found something in my closet to wear.

I decided to wear a pink velour tracksuit, it was so cute. For my perfume, I sprayed on Prada Candy. I smelled delectable in my opinion. I rushed out of the house to make it on time to meet my BFF. I finally reached the train station and took the train to meet Veronica. I was looking all over for her and finally I saw her staring me down and waving for me to come over.

"Girl, I missed your physical presence in my life," she said.

I smiled and gave her the biggest hug. We walked to the nail salon. On our way there, we were talking about which nail design we'd get. All I knew was it had to be pink. Veronica said it didn't matter to her, she'd pick a color on a whim. We entered the nail salon and saw a woman waxing someone's eyebrows. As soon as our eyes locked, she asked what service we would like, and I said I wanted a manicure and pedicure. She called over two ladies and they took us to the back.

They had pedicure spa chairs over there. We both sat down in the chairs and waited for the ladies doing our nails. They came back with the nail color swatch set. I already knew I was getting pink, but I wasn't sure which kind. I decided on a light baby pink. Veronica looked at the color swatch and chose a lilac purple shade. As our nails were being done, Veronica and I started talking.

"Afua, so are you gonna tell me about that ring on your finger?"

I completely forgot it was on my finger. "Jeremy got me a promise ring after our cooking date."

"Okay sis, you have a wonderful guy. Things aren't going well with me and Aiden. After he asked me to be his girlfriend, he changed. I'm worried that he might not be interested in me anymore."

"Why do you feel this way? Do not to allow your insecurities to break up a chance at a good relationship. Who knows, he might be going through some stuff you have no idea about, but that's still no excuse."

"I barely get to talk to him and fear he's talking to someone else."

"Have you brought it up to him?"

"No," Veronica said.

"You should tell him how you're feeling. If all of this continues, you really need to reevaluate whether you should be dating him."

She received my advice well, but I could tell she was disappointed by his actions. Before we knew it, our toes were done. The ladies helped us put our shoes on, which I felt was kind of them. They brought us to the nail station and asked us what style we wanted. I scrolled through Pinterest and stumbled across a long coffin heart pattern nail design. I showed it to the woman doing my nails. She began working on them. Veronica had an idea of what she wanted, which was a long coffin glitter design.

Our conversation shifted to talking about Thanksgiving, because it happened to be tomorrow.

"All I know is my mom went shopping yesterday for the food we'll be eating."

Veronica's family had already started prepping the food for tomorrow. "I will be helping my mom cook, as I do every year." Veronica was the only child. She always wanted another sibling, but it never happened. We ended up talking about old times in high school.

"Veronica, do you remember that time it was senior skip day, and we actually went to school?"

"Yes, a teacher had to tell us to leave early and enjoy our day."

I realized now that I was really into my studies and going to school. That was a funny moment. "I also remember when people talked about you not going to prom. I didn't understand why people cared so much."

"Exactly. It was the talk of that school. Even people I didn't know were coming up to me asking why."

I told them I wasn't interested, but looking back I should've just gone with Veronica. She had so much fun and even went to the after party. We were talking so much that we forgot our nails were finished until we were told. The cost for each of our nails was $110, which nearly gave me a heart attack, but we paid for it and left. I suggested that we should go to Chick-Fil-A, and Veronica agreed. We walked over and placed our order. I ordered a grilled chicken club sandwich, waffle fries, and a cookies n' cream milkshake. Veronica got a spicy chicken sandwich, waffle fries, and a vanilla milkshake. We stepped aside to wait for our food. Once we received our order, we found a place to sit.

I looked at my nails and was in awe of them. They were nice and done well. Veronica also liked her nails. After that, we walked to the train station and went our separate ways after a much-needed hug. After a semi-long train ride, I was finally home. I opened the door said hello and walked my happy self upstairs. I could hear footsteps behind me, and it was none other than Kwabena. He stopped me on my way to my room.

"Wait! Afua. Can I talk to you?"

"Sure, what do you want?"

"I am very sorry for what I said. I didn't mean to say terrible things about your boyfriend buying you a promise ring."

"I forgive you, as long as you don't continue that behavior."

I went into my room and fell asleep, I was super-duper tired. I woke up the next morning feeling like I overslept. I thought I missed a class or something, then reality hit me that I was home. My mom knocked on my door and said it was time to prepare the food and start cooking. She gave me enough time to shower, brush my teeth, and get dressed.

I was dreading going downstairs, for some reason. It pained me to be the only one cooking with my mom, while Chloe and Penelope sat around doing nothing. They usually helped, but only after you practically begged them and right now, I was having none of it. My mom told me I'd make the meat pie. I started by cutting up the potatoes and cooking them until they're al dente. I cooked the corned beef in a pan with onions and seasoned it. I got the flour, salt, baking powder, and one cup of margarine in a bowl and mixed it until I could start kneading the dough. To the corned beef, I added the potatoes and scallions. I separated the dough and pressed them out with a rolling pin. I filled each of the flattened circles with the corned beef mixture and sealed it with water around the edges. Finally, I used a fork to seal it further and used an egg wash over the pies. It took 20-30 minutes to bake the pies on 350°F. I also made mac and cheese and fried chicken.

My mom made bofrot and party style jollof rice with goat meat. She also made salad and bought a cake. In addition to this, we got assorted drinks, such as soda and juice. As a family, we got dressed up and went to the dining room once the food was set up on the table. We were all wearing forest green. The guys in the house wore green shirts while the girls wore dresses. I picked out a turtleneck flounce sleeve dress with pleats and a belt. My mom told us to take a family picture. We got the tripod and set her phone on it. I got the tripod remote and used it to take pictures. They all came out looking amazing. We then went to the dining table and sat down. My mom wanted us to pray as a family before eating. She always says this quote by Mahalia Jackson that says, "Faith and prayer are vitamins of the soul; man cannot live in health without them."

This year, it was Penelope's turn to lead prayer. She said, "Thank you God for the food we are about to eat and let it fill our bodies. We thank you for the fact that we get to be here surrounded by loved ones. In the name of Jesus I pray, amen."

We all said the "May the grace of our Lord Jesus Christ" prayer and then we began eating. The food was so delicious. I was especially proud of myself for making some of the food. Everyone complimented me on making the meat pies. I felt blissful. It was a great time being with family. We shared good news with one another. Kwabena decided which college he'd like to attend, which was Binghamton University. Penelope and Chloe were both getting good grades, and my dad got a promotion at his job in tech. My mom was doing well at the hospital she worked for, and had been praised by her supervisors. Everyone had something good to say, which was uplifting. We were full from our dinner, so my mom suggested we play a game about all the things we were grateful for. It could be a memory, place, or person. We each took turns and shared the memories we had with one another. I talked about the time we went to Luna Park at Coney Island. It was fun; we got on the rides and had ice cream after. We also played Monopoly for the rest of the night. Family was essential to one's growth. I was a living testimony of that. I was glad I had great people in my corner.

Queen

Maame Yaa finished Jeremy's and my outfits for the African Student Organization's event. This woman really came through for me. It was very expensive, but knowing her work, it was worth every penny. I picked up the dress at the main lobby desk. At first, I was confused as to why I got an email saying I had a package. Then I realized it was my outfit and I was filled with delight. I practically ran to my room and put on the dress. I needed help zipping the dress up. Luckily Melissa was there to assist me. As soon as I put it on, I was amazed; it was so beautiful. It was all red with intricate beading. In Ghana, they call the top and bottom a kaba and slit.

Melissa saw me and said, "Afua, you are going to be a show-stopper in that dress. I wish I could go, but I have finals to study for."

I took it off and placed it on a hanger in my closet. I was shocked that the event was tomorrow. I guess I got it in the nick of time. I called Jeremy and told him that his clothes arrived. I could tell by the sound of his voice he was thrilled to see how his clothes looked. I asked him what time he would stop by my room. He said he'd come later when he was done with work.

In the meantime, I sat at my desk and practiced the story I would tell in sign language. I stuck to the flower girl one. I'd practiced so much that it all came naturally.

A little while later, I got a knock on my door and it was Jeremy. I showed him his outfit and he was happy about the quality and style. It had buttons on the front and was designed in a unique pattern.

As soon as he saw it, he said, "Wow, I'm going to look dapper." I finally showed him my dress and he could barely speak— all he said was, "A true queen."

I started giggling. I said I would need him to take me to a girl named Neriah that lives off campus tomorrow morning to do my hair.

"Have you eaten anything yet?" he asked.

"No, not since morning."

He offered to order me some food, which I accepted because I was not turning down a free meal. He gave me his phone and it was on DoorDash. I looked through the food places and selected Burger King.

"Do you want anything?"

"No, I ate earlier with some friends," he said.

I continued ordering my food. I got a bacon melt medium meal with pink lemonade. I wanted to get a shake but figured it would be too much. It was a good thing that he asked me if I ate, because my stomach was growling, and I couldn't take it anymore. He waited for me to get my food and walked with me back to my dorm, where we sat and just talked while I ate. Jeremy asked me how preparing for my finals was going. It hadn't been bad for me because I'd been preparing for almost a week. I was more concerned about my sign language final. Jeremy said he was a bit stressed out about his classes, but knew that he would pass. I just listened and told him that he could do it. I reminded him about the sermon from my church. Having faith was essential to succeeding in life. He asked me what style I was thinking of doing my hair.

I said "Me hene (my king), it's going to be a surprise and no hints either, or it will spoil it."

He started pouting and begging me to tell him, but I wouldn't budge. He was over there saying he didn't like surprises and I said, "Well, you going to like this one."

Eventually, he just gave up and said, "I'm sure you'll look beautiful, my Nubian goddess."

That's when I started laughing, because he'd never called me that before. We talked until it was around 10 pm, when Jeremy left. He was getting tired. I could tell by the way he was yawning every few minutes. He told me that he'd meet me in the main lobby tomorrow at 9 am. I fell asleep shortly after he left. I didn't even get to watch my favorite shows first. I guess I was more tired than I expected. I woke up feeling happy because my hair was about to be slayed. I got ready and called Jeremy to drive me off campus. He said he'd be downstairs in five minutes. A few minutes later he knocked on my door and we were on our way to my hairstylist.

She lived in the Auden Albany apartment complex. I heard that they have a fitness gym, game room, and study lounge. I might consider living there after next school year; who knows, maybe I could move in with some friends. My parents would flip out if I decided to move in with Jeremy. They'd say, "You know that living with your boyfriend will cause sexual immorality." Then they would say, "Afua, the only time you move in with your significant other is when you're married." My parents were old school and didn't play those games.

We arrived at the apartments, and I sent a text to Neriah. She came downstairs shortly after. She greeted me but I could tell she was a bit distant, but I brushed it off. Maybe I was bugging and she was actually nice. We took the elevator to the second floor. We turned the corner, and her apartment was right there. She lived in a three-bedroom apartment with roommates. It was a nice set up, if you asked me. She told me we would be in her room. I followed behind her and went inside. Her room was decked out in lilac.

She really was organized. She had me sit in the chair in front of her vanity. Neriah asked me for the wig I'd be using and began working on my hair. It was very quiet, like you could cut the tension with a knife.

I tried to make conversation. "Neriah, what's your major?"

She paused for a second and said, "I'm in my junior year and my major is human development."

It was quiet for a few more minutes before I asked another question. "So, what do you plan on doing in that field?" I said.

"I want to become a marriage and family therapist."

"That's cool! I would like to be a psychotherapist."

That's what got the ball rolling with our conversation. She then told me that she heard about me and Jeremy through Juliet, and she had misconceptions about me because of her. Juliet told Neriah that I was weird and that Jeremy would break up with me and discard me like trash. She also said that I was stupid for thinking that Jeremy could date a girl like me. Neriah apologized for allowing Juliet to get in her head. I forgave her because I knew Jeremy's ex would be a problem.

I told Neriah that I met Juliet, but she was being very rude towards me. She even tried to get with Jeremy, but he turned her down.

She said, "Really? I had no clue. Anyways, don't pay her any mind. She's only bitter that things didn't work out for her relationship wise since the breakup." She told me how the African Student Organizations events are one of the biggest occasions on campus. She inquired about what I would wear. I showed her a picture and she said, "Girl, you are going to look fabulous. I can't wait to see it in person."

She showed me her dress. It was a rose-pink color, and it was off the shoulder. We talked so much until she was finally done. Did I forget to say what hairstyle it was? Oh, my bad. I had a pin curl bun updo with a side bang. I texted Jeremy and told him I was done, and he picked me up. He didn't recognize me at first. He just drove past me. I called him and he drove back around.

When he saw me, he said I was beautiful and that sparkle in his eyes was there. I felt warm inside and all my worries went out the window. He drove us back to the dorms and we walk to my room. It was 12:15 pm and I had enough time to get ready. I went into my fridge and got something to eat. I couldn't find anything, so I settled on a chocolate chip PopTart. I sat and thought about life and how this semester was coming to an end. So many things happened in just a few months. I couldn't believe we were approaching finals. I wondered if I would be victorious despite the two weeks I was behind in work. College was rough and if you didn't take care, you could lose your sanity trying to keep up. I sat there in silence, just stuck with my thoughts. Then a tune came in my mind that I couldn't seem to shake. It's the Brandy song titled "Sittin' Up in My Room." I began humming the chorus to myself. I was so lost in thought that I didn't realize an hour had passed. By that time, it was around 1:15 pm. I told myself that by 2:30 pm, I would start getting ready. In the meantime, I just watch some good old TV shows.

I watched *Family Matters* and I was in '90s nostalgia. I watched the episode where Myra and Steve broke up and he went to Laura's house. Myra barged in and tried to win Steve back, but her attempt didn't work, and she told him she wouldn't back down. As soon as I finished that episode, I was on a binge until it was time to get ready. I changed into my robe and started to work on my makeup. I tried to do a neutral glitter glam look. It came out exactly as I hoped it would. By the time I finished that look, it was 3:00 pm. I knew I had to hurry up. I put on my Victoria Secret Bombshell perfume. I needed help zipping up my dress, but Melissa wasn't around, so I texted Jeremy to see if he was around. Luckily for me, he already finished getting dressed. He came downstairs and helped me get dressed. He was speechless seeing me with my hair and makeup on. He just stood there staring at me with a wide smile.

During that moment, I felt so amazing and self-assured in myself. The level of confidence I had right now was something that I had been striving for since my diagnosis. For once, all the self-doubt just dissipated. Randomly, "Pretty Girl Rock" came in my head, and I began singing. I guess me and Jeremy were in sync because he started to sing right along with me. I guess you could say we were that kind of couple that vibes together. After that I was done getting dressed and it was time to head over to the college center. As I walked outside, I kept getting stares. Someone came up to me, asking where I got the dress made. I gave her the details and told her how great Maame Yaa sewed. Jeremy and I waited on the line for the event. We met up with McKenzie. She gasped when she saw my outfit and kept complimenting me. I appreciated the love I was getting.

The line moved up and we were approaching the front. Once we got there, the girls dealing with the tickets asked for ours, so we showed them our phones. When we went inside, it was nicely decorated in gold. There was a photo booth stand with ASO's logo. At the back of the room, people brought out trays of food. We conveniently found some seats on the second row. We waited for thirty minutes while the room filled up before the event started. The emcee was a woman named Rachel. She was lively and kept the energy going. She announced the ASO dancers onto the floor, which made everyone scream. They start dancing in unison, doing some African cultural dances such as Alkayida, Network, Pilolo, Amapiano, Kupe, etc. The amount of dedication it took for them to be this good was amazing. Once they were done, the contestants of the pageant came out one by one. There were three girls and three guys. The countries being represented were South Africa, Ethiopia, Eritrea, Senegal, Ghana, and Nigeria.

I thought the people represented the countries very well with their traditional wear. After that, they did a segment showcasing different fashion designers from NYC. It was very nice, and some were very creative with their hoodies, dresses, and outfits. They also had a point where a rap duo came and performed. I forgot their names, but it was good. Everyone was vibing to the song they rapped. It was time for intermission. Everyone got up to go and get some food. When I went to the back, there was chicken and fried rice, little sandwiches, cookies, cakes, juice, etc. There was such a wide selection of food that I didn't know what to pick. I eventually settled on chicken and fried rice. I kept on getting stares by people and they were whispering amongst themselves.

Neriah came up to me and said, "What a wow, you look gorgeous and so does the dress."

I smiled. "Thank you!"

"I need your tailor for the next event I go to," she said.

I gave her the details and she was cheerful. I went to sit down and ate a little when they started the best-dressed segment.

The host Rachel went into the audience and started grabbing people to come on the stage. I was one of the people called. I just remembered feeling nervous and that my stomach was in knots. There were like four of us there, two girls and two guys. We each model-walked across the stage. I was scared I'd trip and fall, but I did well. I showcased the beauty of the dress. The host had the audience scream for who was best dressed. Long story short, I was the one that the audience chose. I was so filled with joy, nobody could take that away from me. They played DJ Spinall featuring Mr. Eazi Ohemaa, and the crowd went wild. So, you can imagine how I felt. I walked to that song and did some twirls.

Rachel asked me who did my dress, and I shouted out, "Maame Yaa."

They gave me a $50 Visa gift card for winning, it was a great moment for me. One of the highlights from this semester. I got off the stage and headed back to my seat, and all eyes were on me. It felt good to win, but most importantly, it boosted my confidence.

Jeremy told me how great I was on stage. He said I looked so poised and self-assured. I actually didn't know where that energy came from, I guess I was feeling myself. It was now time for the contestants to showcase their talents. The contestant from Ghana did a skit about a child wanting to pursue her dream of being a singer, but her mother said that singing wasn't a career, and she should pick a realistic job. When she sang, it was heavenly. I thought for sure she was going to win, but the queen ended up being Eritrea and the king was Senegal. Overall, the event went well, and the food was good. Someone announced that there was an after party and we should buy some tickets to get in. Jeremy didn't hesitate to buy two tickets for the both of us. We walked back to our dorm. I changed out of my dress, put on a beautiful outfit, and headed to the main lobby to meet Jeremy and McKenzie. Jeremy drove us to where the after party was located. We luckily got there before they started turning people away at the door.

We randomly saw Gabriel at the party. Well, he spotted us first. I was surprised to see him, being that we did not get a chance to speak during the show. He was part of the board members and was behind the scenes making sure the show ran smoothly. He was with a girl with freckles, tan skin, and beautiful curly hair.

Jeremy gave him a pound, saying, "My son got a girl. No wonder I haven't seen much of you." He just began laughing.

The vibes were there at the party. They were playing all the old African tunes like "Premier Gaou" by Magic System and "Old Man Boogey" by FBS. Everyone was enjoying themselves and jamming to every song the DJ played. He really knew how to get the crowd dancing. There was a circle forming and people took turns showing their best moves in the middle. I would've gone if I wasn't so shy. That night was amazing, I kept singing my heart out to all the songs being played. We legit didn't leave until like 2:30 am. That was the latest I'd been out in a while, but it was well worth it.

The next morning, I had the worst headache, and it didn't help that I had a call from my Auntie Patricia. She was the aunt I avoided talking to at all costs. She was argumentative and very cutthroat with her words. She never saw her faults and thought because she was older than my mom, she had the final say. Someone told her that I was hospitalized and diagnosed with bipolar disorder and depression. I wondered how she found out; I bet it was my parents or Akosua. She then asked me why nobody told her this. I didn't know what to say, I was taken aback. *It's because you're judgmental and rude,* I thought. She also said that I should pray harder, that it was because I didn't have faith in God. That was the reason why evil spirits took ahold of me and caused this to happen.

I was highly offended. I wanted to scream at her and tell her my mind, but all I could do was cry. Did she know how much I struggled with depression? Did she even care? Oh, wait I guessed not. She would just tell me I brought this onto myself. Those were things left unsaid. I didn't want to confront her, I just took it. I don't know why I didn't defend myself; maybe I was scared. I kept thinking, *What about caring for my well-being? Why must she be so careless with her words?* She asked me if I was listening to her and when I said yes, she rambled on and on about religion and how fundamental prayer was. I couldn't reason with people like her. She had a fixed mindset on this matter. Aunt Patricia's character is bad; in Twi that translated to, "ne suban nyɛ papa." Those words of hers would affect my interactions with her moving forward. I didn't know why I gave her such power.

Eventually I wiped away my tears and said nothing. She just told me that if I kept on taking medication, eventually I'd be dependent on it and that I needed serious prayer to be delivered from this. That it was not normal for someone like me to all of a sudden have mental issues. I really was tired of people treating mental illness like it was something to be delivered from. I wondered if she even knew that what she was saying only made her sound ignorant. It was an imbalance in my brain, something that medication was helping me overcome. I was well aware that I'd be on this treatment plan for the rest of my life. I didn't need to hear it, and the more she talked, the more I wanted to hang up the phone and block her.

She later got the hint that I didn't want to talk to her. Aunt Patricia said, "Okay, I will leave you to work on your studies. Please take heed to what I said." And then she hung up.

Lucky for me, my roommate was gone and didn't have to witness me crying. I called my mom to tell her what happened. My mom told me how sorry she was about my aunt disrespecting me. I asked my mom why Aunt Patricia hated me so much. Ever since I could remember, she'd always been negative towards me. It was like nothing I could do was good enough for her.

My mom said, "Afua, I don't think she dislikes you. Unfortunately, that's the way she is." My mom has told me this since I was little, but there was no excuse for my aunt's behavior. I told my mom that I felt like sometimes that was a serious burden on my life. My mom said, "Possibly the very thing we are hiding from is our true self. You have to tap into who you are, Afua. You were made to stand out. Don't let this circumstance pull you away from your destiny." I felt like I had to hide who I truly was from the world. I was learning that I didn't have to anymore.

My mom said she'd talk to my aunt. I pleaded with her not to because it was all going to come crashing on me. She would yell at me even more, then say I couldn't fight my own battles. My mom assured me she wouldn't, but told me that I shouldn't let people's words get me down. It was easy for her to say; she didn't have to live with this. I did. She prayed for me and then hung up. I decided I would get up and start studying for finals. I figured that would get my mind off of how I was feeling at the moment. I studied for my psychology final. My professor made it eighty questions long, focusing on everything we learned since the start of the semester. I figured I'd text Rochelle and ask her if she would like to study. She said yes and that she was struggling to remember the concepts from the beginning of the semester. I was a bit uneasy about the test despite the fact that I knew the topics very well. I got my flashcards and made a Quizlet so that I could study on the go. I told Rochelle that I would send her my Quizlet so she could study too. I felt the same way about my math final, being that it wasn't my strong point.

When I finish my Quizlet, I started studying the questions. It was cool being able to relearn all the concepts I learned for these past few weeks. I couldn't believe I knew most of the terminology. I realized that math was more important to study for, so that was what I did. I was doing algebra which got confusing, so I texted Jeremy and asked him for help. He was happy to help me solve the problems and explained to me how he got to the answer. We spent the rest of the day working on math problems while Jeremy prepared for his final exams. He told me how demanding and time consuming his finals were. He had to frequently study if he wanted to keep up with his classes. Jeremy told me about General Chemistry 2 and how difficult it could be if you weren't studying efficiently. I asked if he wanted to pray with me so that God could guide us through our exams. I prayed for God to allow for us to retain the information we were studying for our finals.

"God, please give us guidance and understanding. Everything that we learn, may it be on the test and may we know the correct answers. We thank you for bringing us this far. I hope you continue to protect us, in Jesus' name we pray, amen."

Then I touched my Gye Nyame necklace and remembered what Jeremy said—that in my toughest moments, God was there. We studied for a little more before we felt burnt out and agreed to stop. I was tired. So, after Jeremy left, I just fell asleep. I didn't even bother thinking about the food I was going to eat. Sleep came over me. Plus, I had to work the next morning. The library was staying open twenty-four hours. Each worker had to pick up some shifts. I was able to choose two outside of my normal hours. I woke up and got ready as I usually would for work. I grabbed a PopTart and ate it on my way to the library. Somehow, my mind started thinking about what happened yesterday with my Aunt Patricia and it set me in a bad mood. I thought about the words she told me. *"It's because you don't pray."* I thought, *what does she know about me?*

Normally when I was down, I wrote my feelings on the notes section of my phone. I typed until I couldn't anymore.

> I want to tell you that I'm more than my diagnosis. I'm human. Yes, I have my shortcomings, but who doesn't? You see me trapped inside my own thoughts thinking when will this all be over? Those which consume my mind on a regular. Yet you turn my pain into your gain. Had me calling myself crazy 'cause of your narrow mindset. You use my struggles and turn them into an attack. I take it personally, and you just say, "Get over it." Only to throw it in my face again. When you see me, you see someone that needs deliverance. How can I be delivered from something that's probably innate? We all struggle with something, mine just happened to be overt at one point and time. Don't label me because of your misunderstanding of who I am. Let me reintroduce myself and let you know your labels don't define me.

I came to the realization that she knew nothing about me. She might be family but that didn't mean I had to keep her in my life. Everything she thought about me was irrelevant. She was saying things about me that should be told to her kids. They didn't practice their faith, and last time I heard, her son Micah was an atheist. He practically told everyone that, and my aunt pretended he didn't exist anymore. She should focus on building a relationship with him before it was too late. I didn't judge people, because everyone's walk in faith was up to them, but this woman pushed me to the edge with those statements. Let me calm down before someone asked me if I was okay. I could feel my face getting tense and frown lines forming on my forehead. I was fuming mad, and nothing could change it. That was until I went into work, and I had to put up a facade like everything was alright. I did my whole shift feeling angry, but like I said, I hid my feelings very well. Everyone assumed I was happy and that was the way I liked it. I practically bolted to my room and took a nap to get over how I was feeling. It worked, because I woke up feeling better.

I prayed to God that he would change my heart posture towards my aunt and anyone that thought like her. I wanted to forgive her because she didn't know how her words affected me. After that, I went to order food before I studied for exams. I ordered some McDonald's and then I started studying. Rochelle and I studied in my lounge for the exam. We were getting a grasp of the concepts at hand which was nice. She said at this rate we were both going to pass. I just noticed that I was forgetting an assignment I had due on Friday. I knew I was missing something, but wasn't sure. It was a creative writing essay about anything of my choosing, like the last assignment but different. It could be a fictional story about aliens, for example. This should be interesting. I was creative but I wondered how it would turn out. It had to be a ten-page short story. After that, Rochelle left and I started practicing my sign language, because I was trying to ace my final at all cost. I was so focused on what I was doing that it didn't occur to me that it was 2 am.

It was tough trying to fall asleep. My brain was active, and I still wanted to do more studying and practicing my sign language. I didn't fall asleep until about an hour later. I woke up feeling fatigued and didn't have the energy to tackle the day. I just sat in my bed for another ten minutes before something prompted me to get up. I remembered my *why* for going to college. I had goals to accomplish. Whether or not I wanted to get up, I had to always think of the end goal in mind. While I got ready, my mind drifted to the thought that I might fail all my classes. I went to the lounge of my dorm, and I saw people also working on finals. I found a table and just sat down. I began working on the creative writing short story. I wrote a story about a magical kingdom, where people were ruled by a woman who had magical powers to heal the sick. That's what I was able to write so far. I was able to get my creativity flowing for a little while before studying for my psych final. The first question that popped up on Quizlet was Maslow's hierarchy of needs. It basically talked about the needs of people and their motivation for doing things based on different stages of needs.

Then I had to name the stages such as physiological, safety, love/belonging, esteem, and self-actualization. The next one was mnemonic devices, which were memory techniques that helped people recall larger pieces of info. That included acronyms, associations, chunking, method of loci and songs/rhymes. I was thinking about utilizing it to help me better study for this exam. The third question had to do with flashbulb memory. I had to name the examples of it. One of them was the Challenger Space Shuttle explosion. The fourth question was about implicit bias. That was a kind of bias that happened unconsciously and unintentionally that affected judgments, decisions, and behavior. Examples of were race and ethnicity, age, gender, LGBTQ+ and ability bias. I was really in the zone studying all my Quizlet questions. I tuned out the whole room.

When it was 11 pm, I got up, packed my stuff, and left. My psych final would be the next day. Surprisingly enough, I wasn't as nervous as I had been. The next morning, I saw Rochelle and she said that she was prepared and felt like we both would pass. We told each other good luck and then Dr. Brown handed us the test. I had reassurance that I would pass when I saw I knew all the answers to the questions being asked. All I could say was thank you Jesus. I was the second to last person to leave the room. I wanted to make sure I didn't miss any questions, and that I answered the short answer questions to the best of my ability. I rewarded myself by getting a strawberry açaí lemonade refresher and two cake pops, one cookies n' cream and the other birthday cake. I was in such a good mood, my smile was infectious and made other people smile just looking at me. I went to my room and worked on my sign language, since my final was the next day. I had perfected my story and learned sign language in the process. I knew that I would do fine if I just took my time and did my best. I just had to remember the rules of sign language.

Afterwards, I worked on studying for math because the final was also tomorrow. I practiced so many problems I grew tired. That is when I started working on my creative writing assignment. In my story, the main character was the queen of a magical kingdom. Her name was Emelia. In addition to her having healing powers, she could also time travel. She went to all types of time periods when she wanted to get away from her mundane life. She hadn't found love because there was no one like her, apart from family. Emelia time traveled in hope that she'd find someone like her one day. I wrote and wrote until I became worn out. I knew I had to get some sleep and wake up early to continue studying. I woke up the next morning feeling unconfident. There was no way I could pass my finals today. I wanted to avoid studying because thinking about it made me feel uneasy. I pushed through that feeling, knowing that it would soon pass.

I got ready and headed to my math class. I entered the room, and everyone was still studying for the exam. I noticed that some people were stressed out about it. I felt indifferent. I knew that as long as I tried my best, that was all I could hope for. No matter the outcome of this test I knew I would be alright. The professor came in and handed out the exam. As he did, he told us to remove everything from our desk. I remembered what Jeremy was teaching me and the techniques he used when solving the problems. The test was challenging overall. My mindset changed from indifferent to stressed. I tried my best, but I wasn't confident that I answered most of the questions right. There was an extra credit question that I thought I answered correctly, but on second thought, maybe not. I was the very last person to leave, which made me feel terrible.

I left the room telling myself, *Afua, you tried your best.* I got some food at the dining hall. I saw Melissa, who was waving in my direction. I went to sit down beside her.

"How are finals going?" I asked her, and boy did she have a field day telling me about it.

"My classes are rough. I didn't expect to struggle so much this semester."

"Tell me about it. It's been a stressful semester."

Melissa didn't realize it would be difficult doing sports and managing school. Then she dropped a bombshell on me. "I will not be coming back to Albany for the next semester."

"If you do not mind me asking, why?"

"Afua, I have been so homesick, and I've had trouble adjusting. Also, I had a pregnancy scare a couple of weeks ago. I concluded that I need to go back home. I already told Noah, and he wasn't happy, but he understood my position on the matter. We will probably continue dating, but I'm not expecting anything out of it. I will be transferring to College of Staten Island next semester." I wanted to comfort her and tell her that things would be okay. I told her that she had to end this semester off strong and that she could do it. Melissa and I left the dining hall, being that we had finals in thirty minutes.

I walked to my sign language class and waited for the final to start. I saw some of my classmates practicing their signs and they looked to be doing so well. My hands were so sweaty, and I felt light-headed. I sat down and practiced signing to myself as well. The professor came in shortly after. He had our names in random order and would call us to the front. He said that we would get our final score after we were done with our story. I was the fourth person to go. The people before me had interesting stories. One girl went to Bali with her family. When my turn came, it was natural to me. I signed my story, and I could tell people were engaged in what I was signing. They even laughed with me during some parts. After I was done, I felt great. It was a feeling that surpassed all understanding. The professor told us each to come to the front and told us our grade discretely. I found out I got an A. That made me ecstatic; nothing could stop the joy I had within. I wanted to tell someone the good news, but I decided to just reward myself by watching my favorite show.

After I finished watching TV, I was relieved because I was done with three out of four finals. I went to my desk and continued writing my creative story. It was coming together really well. My main character ended up finding love and brought the love interest to live with her in the kingdom. He had to decide if he wanted to stay and leave his life behind or go and miss the love he'd been searching for. I can't ruin my story, so I'll leave it to your imagination. I finished it and figured I would revise my story to make it be the best it could be. I told myself that the assignment was going to go well. I went to Blackboard and submitted my short story. I was finished. The feelings were so strong they overcame me, and I began crying. These were happy tears, because I finally finished my first semester of college. I took a deep breath and closed my laptop. No matter the outcome of the rest of my classes, I was ecstatic that it was over. All that was left was for me to get my final grades—and may they be in my favor.

I was in a creative flow, and as a result, I began randomly writing.

Ohemaa, why you dey worry? When the world has taught you, you're nothing more than your accomplishments. All your efforts diminished, because in this world, if you're not society's standards, you mean nothing. You may not be the standard of beauty, but to me, you're captivating. Stunning, even. So beautiful, people die for your features. So why you dey worry? Like the phrase Wo ho yɛ fɛ (you are beautiful), believe it and life will take its turn. Life gets better and you'll see that the very hateful words they have given unto you was all a lie. Words that were meant to hurt now make you realize your worth. You are like diamonds shining towards the brightest light. You are more than what people may say or do to you. The more you listen to others, the more life becomes miserable. You have to give yourself that self-talk of confidence. That sparks a movement because encouraging yourself makes the difference. You're worthy, beautiful and gifted.

Everything you say, God will listen. Your dreams will come true, but my queen, treat yourself with kindness. It hit me that I would be leaving on Saturday to New York City. I got my room cleaned up to the best of my ability. I started packing my clothes into my suitcase, leaving the clothes I would be wearing for the next few days in my dresser.

I fell asleep very eager to go home in the coming days. When I woke up, I was still fatigued and continued to sleep for another three or four hours. My work shift was 9 pm – 2 am. I was dreading that shift, but I was grateful at least I got to make more money than usual. I looked at my phone and it was 2 pm. I couldn't believe I slept so much. This week had been tiring for me. I was so glad it was coming to an end. I went to the dining hall and got some food in my stomach. After that, I waited in my room for my shift to start. In the meantime, I might as well check my online student portal to see if my professors posted my grades. I saw that sign language was up and I got an A. I wanted to scream from the top of my lungs, but all I did was smile. I checked a GPA calculator website to see what I would need to get a 3.8 or better. In order for me to get to my goal GPA, I would have to get three A's and one B+. That would be roughly 3.83, which wasn't bad at all.

I thought that was attainable but honestly, I didn't know, because the two weeks I missed really set me back. The time went by really fast. I got up, grabbed my bag, and went to the library. The library was pretty busy, and people were frantically doing their last-minute studying. I grabbed my vest that had my name plate on it and put it on. The library was kind enough to cater food and drinks for the students. They had muffins, cookies, granola bars, juice, water, tea, and coffee. I grabbed some on my way to my desk. Once I sat down, there was a line of students requesting my help with finding research articles and books. It was a constant cycle of people coming in and out of the library. I overheard someone say they hadn't left the library since the previous day, which meant they slept there as well. Finals were brutally intense, and if you didn't take care, you would crash and burn. I hadn't seen anyone I knew come by the desk yet.

I helped so many people back-to-back. I was glad I got to be of service to them. I did my whole shift without catching a break. I saw Blake and she was stressed out. I told her to calm down and take a breather, that she would do fine with a positive attitude. I was exhausted by the time my shift was over. Lucky for me, my next shift started at 4 pm. That would give me some time to rest. As soon as I was in my bed, I fell asleep. I woke up to a phone call from Mrs. Morgan reminding me about my appointment next month. It was on January the 13th. That meant I would have to drive back up to Albany before school started. I might have to make it an all-day trip, because students weren't allowed to stay on campus without permission during the break. I got ready and stayed in my bed watching TV shows until my next shift. I walked over to the library and saw that they were having a staff party. My employers said we could go one by one upstairs to get some food. Today, not so many students were there; most had left campus or were anticipating winter graduation. An hour into my shift, I got the okay to go upstairs. They decorated the room so nice with balloons and red and green decorations. They had a section full of gifts, with each of our names on it. I looked though the gifts and found mine.

I saw McKenzie there and went over to her. We talked about the semester coming to an end. We had one more semester and our freshman year would be over; how crazy was that? The food selection was pretty good, if you asked me. It was a potluck style. People brought in some food such as chicken, mac and cheese, rice and beans, oxtails, lasagna, sweets, and cake. It was a great selection of food. After I ate, I stayed for like a total of thirty minutes before I had to go back downstairs. I wished I could've stayed longer, but work was important. A few minutes passed and I felt someone approaching me. I was preoccupied by the computer and I didn't notice who it was. I looked up and it was Juliet, right in front of my desk. She asked if we could talk. I was confused, because why would she choose now to speak with me? Especially since I was at work. I said sure. She told me how sorry she was for acting rude towards me. Juliet also said that things had been hard for her since the breakup and when she saw Jeremy had a new girlfriend, she became jealous. I accepted her apology and told her that I respected her for being honest with me. She left and I felt at ease about the situation.

I finished my shift, went to my room, and relaxed. I had some left-over food from the party, which I heated up and ate. I did what I normally liked to do, which was watch TV shows until I got tired. Tonight, I watched *Abbott Elementary,* and it was funny. I only watched a few episodes, because the next morning I would be headed back to NYC. I called Jeremy and confirmed the time we would be leaving, and he said 10 am. I woke up feeling ready to leave. I showered and got dressed. Before I could leave, Stacy had to check my room and make sure it was okay. Then I was able to sign out of my dorm. I waited in the main lounge for Jeremy. I waited another ten minutes before I saw him. I smiled and he gave me a hug, smelling of sweet cologne. He got me in a way that no one else did, which I appreciated. We walked to his car. He grabbed my bags and put them in the back seat. We went to the gas station so Jeremy could get gas. I went into the convenience store and bought a few snacks.

Jeremy wanted to pay, but I used my Visa gift card. We were on the road after that. We were playing songs and singing along for the next two hours. On the final hour, Jeremy told me that he booked a trip for us to go to Montreal, Canada for my birthday. I let out the biggest scream and kissed him on the cheek. I'd never been to

Canada, so that would be fun. He said that we would be going the week of January 16th. I wondered what we'd be doing for my birthday. I had to get my outfits situated for the trip. I told him that I had an appointment on the 13[th,] and he offered to drive me. One thing I liked about my man was that he'd offer to help me out without complaining about it. He would never throw what he did in my face. One of his love languages was acts of service. That was why I loved him more each day. He was a great person and I didn't want to lose what we had.

We approached my house. I was very happy about the break starting and the vacation I'd be going on. Jeremy dropped me off at my house and gave me a big hug. Surprisingly, no one was at home yet. They all went out to do something. He helped me get my suitcase upstairs before leaving. I was energized after that drive. I was not sure why though, I should be tired. I guessed being a passenger queen had its perks. I stayed in my room and spent the rest of the day watching shows until my family came home. They had no clue I was coming today. You can imagine their excitement to see me home. We watched a movie together which happened to be *I Wanna Dance With Somebody*. It was a Whitney Houston biopic. I'd wanted to watch it for some time. The next day went by fast. I went to church, had brunch with my family, and just relaxed the rest of the day. Monday was a very emotional day for me. I woke up feeling good, but my emotions got the best of me when I saw my final grades and overall GPA. I couldn't believe I got two A's, one in Sign Language and Psychology101. Then I got a B+ in English 101 and a B- in Math 101. I cried when I saw those grades because I was used to having straight A's.

My mom was the first person I told. She said, "Afua my dear, you have to give yourself grace. You went through a lot this semester and still managed to get Dean's list. That is a blessing I'm so proud of you."

Once I heard that, I felt a bit better. This year had been full of highs and lows. Everything I went through was for a purpose.

Finding Me

Christmas and New Year's went well with my family. I was grateful for the time I shared with them. I took Jeremy to a karaoke place called Karaoke City NYC. It was so much fun being in our own space singing. We sang "You Gotta Be" by Des'ree and many more. It was a great segway into the new year, after going to church, of course.

Jeremy loved the surprise and said, "Babe, you really thought about me which is nice. I had so much fun. We should do this again."

A few weeks later, I went on that amazing trip with Jeremy. My dad had his reservations, but he ultimately let me go because he knew that I was in safe hands.

I met Jeremy's parents at the airport. They seemed to like me, from what I could tell. They were praising me and saying how I was smart and that Jeremy was lucky to have a girl like me. I saw his sister Naomi. She was so adorable with her two afro puffs. Naomi had beautiful hair and her skin was perfect. She had the teddy that Jeremy made for her; she said his name was Winnie like the character Winnie Pooh. She was happy to see me.

She said, "You're my brother's girlfriend. I think you're so pretty."

That warmed my heart that she also liked me. Jeremy and I took a plane to Montréal. I didn't realize that most people there spoke French. We stayed in the Warwick Le Crystal. It was a beautiful hotel. We were able to get complimentary breakfast. For my birthday, we went sight-seeing around the hotel and did some shopping.

We went to this restaurant called Salumi Vino. The food was good, but not memorable besides the cake I ate. They sang happy birthday to me, which was great. I heard that Canada was famous for their poutine, so I had to try it. My opinion was that it was good. The mixture of the flavors was nice. After that we went to La Cornetteria, which is a bakery. Over there, we tried cronuts. It tasted so delicious. We went sight-seeing and got a tour of old Montréal. In particular, we went to the Pointe-à-Calliére Museum, where we learned about preserved archeological sites. Then we went to the Quebec City tour. The area was very stunning and unique. We took a trip near the Saint Lawrence River (old port) to see the giant Ferris wheel. The views from up there were breathtaking. Finally, we went to the Jardin Botanique (Botanical Garden). I didn't want to leave.

I received a text from Emma saying that she would like to hang out with me. I had to tell her that I was on break and that we could hang when the semester started. I hadn't seen her since I left that hospital. I thought I wouldn't hear from her, but I was glad I did. She was bummed, but understood where I was coming from. Before I started the next semester, I received an email from housing saying I had a new roommate. Her name was Scarlet and she was black. She was from New Jersey and she seemed like a free-spirited person. I couldn't wait to see how well we'd get along. I just hoped there wouldn't be any drama or arguments. Everything that I hoped for had come true. Some things in life had shown me to be humble and have humility. This wasn't the end of my story, but the beginning of a new one full of love and happiness. I finally found myself on the journey to becoming me. I'd been through a lot, but God sustained me and guided me. He can do the same for you. This wasn't a good-bye, but an introduction to what lies ahead.

* * *

Thank you for taking the time out to read my book. I hope you enjoyed it. If you are interested in signing up for my newsletter, I have put the link down below.

https://mailchi.mp/f73d61f4c2cd/aqueensdiaries-email-sign-up

About the Author

The author Mary Mensah received her bachelor's degree from SUNY Plattsburgh in Upstate NY. She majored in psychology with a double minor in gender & women's studies and communication sciences and disorders. She then went to SUNY Oswego where she got her masters in school counseling. In her free time, she loves to watch YouTube and tv shows such as A Different World. She enjoys furthering her knowledge and has a passion for mental health.

instagram.com/aqueensdiaries_96

facebook.com/mary.mensah.35

tiktok.com/@aqueensdiaries_96

youtube.com/@Ohemaamary

goodreads.com/marymensah_96

amazon.com/author/marymensah_96

threads.com/@aqueensdiaries_96

* 9 7 9 8 9 9 9 0 4 0 6 2 3 0 *